Coffee Break with the Billionaire

A CINNAMON ROLLS AND
PUMPKIN SPICE ROM-COM

by

Holly Kerr

Also By

Love in Laandia

Sweet Royal Romance

Royal Rumble
Royal Retelling
Royal Rising
Royal Reluctance
Royal Rebel
Royal Replacement

DEDICATION

To all my readers who wanted more Fenella

READERS EXPECTATIONS

Heat Level: low; holding hands, swoony kisses; minimum swearies

Notable Tropes: cinnamon roll hero, friends-to-lovers, fish out of the water, small town, opposites attraction, billionaire, royalty

Triggers: alcohol use, bad parenting, minor LGBTQ character

Style: first person present, dual POV

Stress Level: low

Ending: HEA

NOTE: I honestly moved heaven and earth for Fenella and Silas. Literally—I took quite a bit of creative license when you can see Neptune and the Draconid meteor shower. Neptune will be in view earlier in the year, as well as the meteors. My apologies... but it works for the story!

SECOND NOTE: Laandia is not a real country. My apologies to the people of Newfoundland and Labrador in Canada for taking your beautiful province (I'm planning a visit in 2025!) and giving it to King Magnus and his Viking ancestors. I'm a writer—I can do things like this!

PROLOGUE

Five years ago...

ONCE UPON A TIME, there was a handsome prince who lived in a far-off kingdom on the edge of the Atlantic Ocean.

The country of Laandia borders the northern part of the Canadian province of Quebec, which lately seems interested in joining the country of Laandia, and the Arctic Circle, which does not want to join any other country because it is too cold for anyone to live there.

The handsome prince from Laandia is dating a girl who happens to be a billionaire.

That girl is me.

The private plane banks as we leave Newfoundland, giving me a first look at the country of Laandia.

Even at this height, it's a colourful sight because the forests that blanket most of the country are now shades of orange and yellow, with a lot of green, plus blue lakes and rivers.

Still—average. Ordinary. I'm not an outdoorsy type. Give me a five-star private resort with a Michelin-starred restaurant and plenty of boutiques in the middle of the woods and I'll be happy, but without it? Meh.

No one else is looking out the window. They're watching my twin brother Ashton throw peanuts into the open mouth of Milo Stapleton-Shak.

"What do you think, Fen?" Gunnar asks. He'd been excited about showing me his home since we started dating a few months ago.

And now I'm finally going to visit Laandia... along with five of my best friends.

I would have been fine travelling with just Gunnar but since this is technically my birthday trip—mine and Ashton's—having friends along makes sense.

"It looks like... land."

My comment doesn't diminish Gunnar's excitement one little bit. "Just wait until you get the first glimpse of Battle Harbour. And the castle. It looks great from the air."

That is what makes Laandia different from other countries, and I've been to a lot of countries. It has a castle. And a royal family who lives there.

There are many countries with monarchies, but none like the Ericksons. King Magnus is like no other king—he was in a rock band. And won a gold medal in one of the Olympics. He has four sons and one daughter, and each one is more beautiful than the last.

I know because I've seen pictures. Also, because I'm dating the youngest son, Prince Gunnar.

I'm dating a prince.

Of course, I'm dating Prince Gunnar of Laandia—daughters of billionaires get those perks.

And it's just fair that we get those perks, because being a billionaire is *hard*. Pictures and videos are being taken constantly; there are lies and rumours, and demands for your time to show up at charities, films and parties. And don't get me started on all the shopping you need to do to be on the leading edge of fashion—which I am.

Luckily, I have people to help with that.

It may sound like we live in a bubble of indulgence, with private planes, luxury vacations, and five-star meals at our fingertips every day, and I suppose we do. I've been *everywhere*—film premieres, Met Galas, parties for Formula One races all over the world. I've stayed in the Ramburgh Palace in Jaipur, Burj Al Arab in Dubai, and Necker Island with Mr. Branson, a friend of my father's.

It's fun. It's amazing. It's sometimes tough, to show the right side of yourself to a world that only wants your left—your bad side. Who wants you to fail.

That's why I have my friends.

They call us the Billionaire Brats, so resentment is alive and well. The six of us have bonded—me and Ashton, heirs to Carrington Toy fortune, Coral, of AAA winery, Lavinia, she of the one name, Viscount Milo, and Rupert, whose father is important in South Africa, but I can't remember what for.

There are a few others, like Mase Stirling, but it's the six of us that stand together.

Gunnar is with us now because of me. He met Ashton at some race and then fell in love with me.

I fell in love with him. At least I'm pretty sure it's love. I've never actually said those words to anyone.

Maybe it'll be Gunnar.

"Look now," Gunnar urges and I turn back to the window. Below is the town of Battle Harbour, designed in a U-shape with an open end at the water.

The Atlantic Ocean looks a little different here than what I'm used to around Long Island. Angrier, and more gray than blue.

But it's the houses I focus on. "They look like Lego," I tell him.

"It's the prettiest place in Laandia. I hope you like it."

"Of course I will because you're here." I put my arms around him, leaning up for a kiss.

It's the eve of my twenty-second birthday and at this moment, I think this is all I'll ever need.

Fenella

I NEED BETTER SHOES.

The man who designed these shoes was a sadist. And it has to be a man because a woman would not do this to other women—squashing baby toes beyond recognition, adding no padding in the sole and even less grip on the bottom, which causes me to skid along the damp pavement as I dash across the street.

A taxi screeches to a halt as I cross against the light, resulting in a long, drawn-out honk from a Maserati sliding by. The driver shouts something incomprehensible out the window, along with finger gestures. I ignore them and continue to cross because cars will stop for me because I'm Fenella Carrington and things always happen for me.

Except for this. This can't be happening to me.

The music from Bubbles nightclub chases after me, adding to the sounds of the Las Vegas Strip. This truly is a city that never sleeps because it's lit up to be as bright as day and it's very loud, so the only way to sleep in one of the hotel rooms is to take the penthouse, giving you the right amount of distance from the street, or use a sleep mask/earplug combination.

Fortunately, I have access to all of the above.

"Fenella—wait!"

The voice of my boyfriend/fiancé/ex-everything calls after me. Tiger Brannon is a singer and can project his voice over the white noise of the city. I consider that to be his only talent at this moment.

"For what?" Forgetting I'm in the middle of a busy street after midnight, I whirl around to face Tiger, who is panting after me.

You'd think a rock star would have better cardio, but in reality, Tiger is in horrible shape, skinny to the point of scrawny with no visible muscle tone. He's the lead singer for Opium and a fairly boring one at that. He never moves, just clutches the microphone like my friend Gigi when you give her a bottle of Dom Perignon and wails into it.

He is no prince.

Yes, I dated a prince, and unfortunately, every other man I've dated since has been found lacking in comparison. It's not that I want Prince Gunnar back—it's been years, and I pride myself in never going back, only forward—but Gunnar was one of the good ones.

"What should I be waiting for?" I shout at Tiger. Okay, it's more of a shriek than a shout, but I'm an emotional woman and this has been a very bad night.

Three hours ago, I had been in Los Angeles, enjoying sushi with my friends Coral and Rupert when I got the Google Alert that Tiger was at Bubbles, the nightclub owned by my friend, and fellow billionaire, Mase Stirling. The last time I spoke to Tiger, he had been finishing up a show in Dallas, Texas and moving on to the next stop on his tour.

I am not Travis; I would not follow Taylor from show to show. I do like to go once in a while, but Opium is not Taylor Swift. They may have an amazing music video, starring me and two of my model friends, but in my opinion, the band doesn't have the stamina to last, nor have they garnered the celebrity fans to make every concert a must-see event.

But I pride myself on being a good girlfriend. I sprang into action when I found out Tiger was in Las Vegas instead of the Midwest. From the sushi place, I made a few calls and quickly had the Carrington jet fueled and ready to whisk me away to Vegas. Rupert and Coral refused to come with me, even going so far as to point out how Tiger never told me he was less than two hours away by plane, but I still insisted on surprising him.

Bad idea all around. I do wish I could have convinced at least Coral to come because I could really use a squad with me. I'm alone out here for this.

Except for the groups of photographers *there* in front of Bubbles, and over *there* by the casino. They always seem to be around for times like this.

"For you to make out with other women?" I hold up three fingers. "In one night? Did you think I wouldn't find out?"

There are a lot of things I'm only now finding out about Tiger.

Google Alerts followed me from LA; by the time I landed, a handful of photos had shown up on the Internet of *my* boyfriend having some close contact with other women. According to Instagram, two were random fans who happened to be in the right place at the right time to get close to Tiger, but I recognized Luna Birch in the last picture. She's part of a group that follows the band across the country from show to show. Tiger and the band laugh at the group in private, but in the picture splashed across social media, Tiger is too busy exploring Luna's tonsils with his tongue to be laughing.

Because the world knows I'm with Tiger, I got tagged in all the pictures.

Nice of people to want to share the infidelities of my fiancé.

The sprinkle of rain has picked up, adding to the general crappiness of the night. These shoes are not meant for this weather, a surprise for Las Vegas, but neither is what I'm wearing—my Stella McCartney purple velvet flares and brand-new vest, which isn't really a vest but mesh covered in Swarovski crystals. It sparkles prettily in the headlights, but also moulds to my torso when it's wet.

Of course I didn't bring a jacket because that's what drivers are for, to keep you out of the rain.

More cars are stopping and there are many arms, with phones, hanging out of these cars as Tiger is recognized.

Which makes it worse because no one is recognizing me. I'm famous too. Granted, it's more for my father's money, but I've been on the cover of forty-six magazines and have over seventeen million followers, so hello—look at me!

That makes me sound vain, and I'm not that self-absorbed. I'm just really mad at Tiger.

Tiger catches up and reaches out a tattoo-covered hand to me. "Babe."

I jerk away, stepping back into the path of an oncoming car, which swerves around me. There is more shouting and a scream of excitement. Another fan. "Don't babe me. Three girls? And Luna Birch?"

"I don't know what you're talking about." Tiger tries hard to sound innocent but the guilty expression on his face says differently.

"Are you an idiot? I saw the *pictures*. Luna posted all about you kissing her! What are you thinking?"

"Fenella!" A woman shrieks from across the street. "I love you!"

I smile and wave but turn back to Tiger with a frown.

"I didn't think we were exclusive." Tiger holds out his hands with an appealing smile. And he *is* appealing if you like a gaunt frame covered in tattoos and piercings. His eyes are a strange silver-green, his lips are full—albeit with a double hoop on the bottom one—and the shock of platinum hair suits him.

He's the lead singer of the band with the most downloaded song on Spotify this month. Tiger is appealing.

At least he was.

I hold up my hand with the three-karat, square-cut pink diamond ring that Tiger presented me with nine days ago. Nine days! "Not exclusive?" I parrot. "What do you think this means?"

I shriek the last part, like a hyper fangirl. But it's still not enough, so I take off the ring and throw it at him. It bounces off his cheek. And leaves a scratch.

"Jesus!" Tiger slaps a hand on his cheek before scrambling for the ring. It's so big that it's not hard to find on the street.

"Babe. Fenella. You're making a scene," he pleads.

"Yes, and I'm very good at it." A group of teens passes us, not even bothering to hide the fact they're filming this. One of them has a bottle of Pepsi, and I grab it from his hands. He gapes at me as I give the bottle a good shake and spray it all over Tiger.

Now Tiger is the one shrieking as the cold carbonated soda drenches his expensive shirt. "You should write a song about me. Like you promised. Only now it's going to be about an angry ex-fiancée!"

I push the now half-empty bottle of Pepsi back at the guy with an apology and a hundred-dollar bill I had in my back pocket.

And then I walk away, leaving Tiger in the middle of the street.

Taylor Swift would write the heck out of this song.

SILAS

"AN EXTRA PUMP OF pumpkin spice, please, Silas. And ooh, those cinnamon rolls do look good this morning. One of those, too, please."

I am not exceptionally fond of pumpkin spice.

I don't like pumpkin spice and I like everything: rain on Sunday mornings, coffee breath and the way tourists leave Canadian pennies in the tip cup.

Just means there's more to go in the jar at home.

From September 15 to American Thanksgiving, there is a cloud of anticipation every time the door to Coffee for the Sole opens. It's autumn and customers want to put an extra pump of pumpkin spice into everything—coffee, hot and cold, chai tea, regular tea, and even matcha. That combination should be illegal in the coffee shop world.

Here in Laandia, we get a lot of good things from our Canadian and American neighbours, but in my opinion, pumpkin spice is not one of them.

I add two extra pumps to Mrs.McKibbon's low-fat latte with oat milk and unicorn foam and cringe at the smell. Autumn is a beautiful time of the year—and a short one—with the colourful leaves creating a picture-perfect background anywhere you look and the skies near perfect for star-gazing. Here in Battle Harbour, we're so far north that we average about six weeks for fall, from the time the leaves begin to turn to expecting snow before Halloween.

The steady stream of tourists who come for whale-watching and to gaze lovingly at the castle, home of the Laandian royal family, may dry up in the fall, but the townspeople with their obsession with pumpkin-spice everything, more than make up for the loss of tourist business.

Of course, the steady stream of those from away begins again with the first snowfall; the ski resorts north of the town are popular and there are many who will brave the cold wind blowing in from the Atlantic to wander the streets of Battle Harbour, trying to catch sight of one of the members of the royal family. Tourists come in for coffee and gallons of hot chocolate, and for a taste of our famous unicorn froth, and at that time of the year, there is no one asking for their drink to be extra flavoured with a vegetable spice.

But that is weeks away. Until then, it's pumpkin spice time.

"Did you see this?" Leodie thrusts her phone in my face as I slide a sleeve onto the cup. "Fenella Carrington!"

"And?" Yes, my heart gives a stupid thump at the sound of her name but it's nothing like Leodie's excitement. Fenella Carrington is a... I'm not sure what she is. Socialite? Super-model? Internet darling?

Billionaire.

I know she's beautiful, with a sheet of black hair and fascinating eyes that seem to be an actual shade of purple. I know she probably smells of some exotic concoction of flowers and fresh air and—

I may have a crush on a woman who's in an advertisement selling handbags.

Sad.

I may have a crush on her, but Leodie is a fangirl, way worse than I am, and because of this, I indulge her. "What are you showing me?" I ask her because the way she jumps around I can't focus on her phone.

"She threw a bottle of Pepsi at some guy! And a diamond ring. And it wasn't some guy, it was Tiger from Opium, so I guess they've broken up. Did you know she was engaged?" She finishes with a note of accusation in her tone.

Leodie is my mother's sister-in-law's second cousin—everyone is related here in Battle Harbour—and has been working with me at Coffee for the Sole for a little over a year. She's been a big help with her ideas and her energy, but the energy gets a little much sometimes.

"I don't actually know her," I remind my second-in-command.

Fenella Carrington is a friend of Prince Gunnar and has visited Laandia twice, that I know of. She seemed to have a liking for my coffee, so she was in here every day while she was in town, but seeing her that often doesn't mean I *know* her, just enough to develop an unhealthy fascination with a woman because she smiled at me.

It might not be unhealthy; it's not like I'm obsessed with her like Leodie, who follows every social media account Fenella has and keeps griping that she never got to serve her. I just think she's... I don't know what I think. She seemed a bit standoffish and pretentious, but she's the daughter of a billionaire and hangs out with royalty, so what can you expect?

Prince Gunnar is a good guy. All the princes are. Everyone in Battle Harbour knows them, but I wouldn't say I'm close friends with any of them.

They live in a castle. I live in a run-down apartment and run a coffee shop. There is a divide, just as much as there is between Fenella Carrington and me. I am aware of this, which means it's fine that I think she's pretty.

Very pretty.

It's not like anything would ever happen between us.

Leodie rolls her eyes. I've noticed she's big on eye-rolling, and it's very dramatic because Leodie has very big eyes. Velvety brown with coats of mascara, all behind a pair of green glasses which somehow enlarges them even more.

She's very dramatic as well, which can get a little exhausting at times but is mostly fun because I'm pretty low-key. It takes a lot for me to react, and that drives Leodie a little crazy. At least that's what she keeps telling me.

There's not a lot to react to in Battle Harbour. It's a fishing village, on the edge of the Atlantic, neighbours to the Arctic

Circle. Our claim to fame is being the prettiest town in all of Laandia for ten years running, our pub-to-population ratio is impressive, and Coffee for the Sole, which I own, brews the best coffee in the Maritimes.

The daily lineups do give it some merit.

Battle Harbour's claim to fame is definitely the castle.

The castle at the top of the cliff overlooking the town, from where the king of Laandia rules our fair country.

King Magnus, and his four sons and one daughter.

There are quite a few singles that stop by Battle Harbour to throw their hat in the ring, trying to nab a royal.

This is where Fenella Carrington comes back into play. She nabbed one of the royals for a time. I've never had an acrimonious breakup, but I've never been such good friends with one of my exes like Gunnar and Fenella.

It's nice to see in this world where scandals and holding grudges seem to be the norm.

"Looks like she dumped him good," Leodie says, still studying her phone.

"Is there any other way to dump someone? Morning, Sophie." I smile as the woman steps up to the counter. "Usual?"

"Please."

Sophie likes a flat white—espresso with a layer of micro-foam. I make a point to know all the regulars and remember their preferred drinks. I've been at the helm of Coffee for the Sole for almost ten years, after a heart attack caused my father to retire and cut short my post-secondary career. I was fine leaving the University of Laandia to come back here—I may be a small business owner, but I have no love for studying business.

Astronomy is my jam, but I do okay with the shop.

I took what my parents had built and made it better, taking the tired cornerstone of the town square and updating everything—the dishes and décor, the brands of tea, and bringing in a supply of almond and oat milk that my father refused to stock. I splurged on a Victoria Arduino espresso maker that I may still be paying for to this day.

Coffee for the Sole is now the first stop for tourists visiting Battle Harbour. We have a Facebook page and an Instagram account, thanks to Leodie.

Leodie asks Sophie about the Fenella video because, apparently, Sophie is now friends with Fenella. At least she talks about her like she is.

I move on to the next customer. Pumpkin spice latte with three pumps. Americano for the next. Two iced coffees for Rebecca from the bakery.

My dream was to be an astronaut. It's a strange dream for a person who really doesn't like to fly, or do much at a fast speed, and especially odd for someone who lives in a country without a space program. But from the time I was four until I was fourteen, all I wanted was to see the stars.

And then my sister Emily got pregnant.

She was seventeen; it's not unheard of for teenage pregnancies to happen in Battle Harbour, but it is uncommon for teenage parents to run away and leave the baby behind.

With my parents.

My parents—Alister and Betty Bell—had their children later in life, so taking responsibility for their first grandchild in their mid-fifties was a bit of a shock. One day they had been talking about retiring and selling the coffee shop, and the next, my mother had taken a leave to look after Wyatt.

No one ever voiced a word of complaint at the new normal. Of course, we never wanted to see Emily leave, but she had gotten involved with one of the McKibbon boys and not one of the good ones. Rob's family were all fishermen and that wasn't the life he wanted.

Neither was a baby at eighteen.

My sister was young and scared and easy to influence. She was also head over heels in what constitutes as love at seventeen so when Rob suggested the baby would be better off with our parents, it didn't take her long to agree.

At least that's what I think. Emily never talked to me about it. That stung because, before Rob, we had been close; as close as you can be close to your sister who is three years older than you and likes fast cars and drinking Screech with her friends.

Emily liked it when I told her about the stars.

But then she left, running out of town in the middle of the night and leaving four-month-old Wyatt asleep in his crib in her room. My parents gave up their plans of retiring and became his guardians. I gave up my dream of jetting off into space because there was no way I was going to leave my nephew behind after his mother abandoned him.

It wasn't all bad; now sixteen, Wyatt is an amazing kid. And I started studying astronomy on my own. I may never visit the stars, but I certainly know what's up there.

And maybe someday I'll find that person who wants me to tell her about the night sky, but I'm not holding my breath. I have my shop, my friends, family. It's nothing like the bright lights and drama of the TikTok clips that Leodie shows me, but it's a good life.

It's enough.

fenella

Lavinia: should have kept the ring

Coral: champagne would have been better than Pepsi. Except ours, bad publicity

Rupert: whole thing is good publicity for Tiger

Milo: will trash his next song

Lavinia: concert! Fun!

Gunnar: am I allowed to say I have no idea what u saw in him?

Coral: not ur best choice babe

Fenella: I would have appreciated a told you so earlier

Rupert: I think I did

Ashton: I know I did

I send a furious face in response.

No one likes the *I told you* so when they make a mistake, especially of a romantic nature.

And especially when the mistake has been splashed over the internet.

I don't need to scroll through a lot to find the video. Two days after the very public breakup of Tiger and me, it's still the most-watched video on YouTube.

I don't know why—it wasn't even that exciting. I threw the ring and a bottle of Pepsi at him.

Maybe I should have thrown the actual bottle.

Heiress in a snit
Famous for doing nothing.
Temper tantrum terror
Tiger gets blasted.
Meow!

I close my screen. Then I close my eyes. Even though Tiger was in the wrong, no one has picked up on that. He cheated on me. He kissed three different women in one night. And how many would he have stopped at if I hadn't walked in on number three?

And this was the man I wanted as my husband?

In hindsight, maybe I didn't exactly want him as my husband. It was fun being seen with Tiger, especially at his concerts, even though I really didn't love Opium's music. But his tattoos intrigued me and dating him also really upset my mother.

My father hadn't cared one way or another. He was too busy getting the prenup prepared.

I remember when I told them I was dating a rock star. My father was more interested in how much money Tiger earned, but my mother's attention had been entirely on her martini—gin, dry, three olives, marinated in vermouth and with the pits removed.

Only the best for my mother. She takes her martinis seriously, which makes sense since the drink could be a metaphor for her life—dry and a bit salty.

Granted, it wasn't the first time I had told them I was in a relationship with a musician, so that could explain the lack of reaction. But looking back, there hasn't been much of a reaction to anything I do for a while now.

Did I love Tiger? In all honesty, no. Not really. I liked him well enough. Would I have eventually married him? Probably not; but if I'd gone through with it, it would have ended in a quickie divorce, and I darn well would have ensured I got the sympathy for it.

The breakup was a surprise and I wasn't ready for it, which is why I came off as an unhinged shrew.

www.ilovetigeropium.com's words, not mine.

I heave a sigh and set my phone down.

This mess has come too soon after the video of me crowd surfing at the Olivia Rodrigo concert where I accidentally kicked a young fan. I really didn't mean it; someone had grabbed my bum and I kicked out in reflex.

That had been the day after my ranting post on abortion rights had gone viral, and countless comments wondered if I was pregnant. When Tiger had publicly denied it, someone had started the thread about how it wasn't his baby and *WhoisthefatherofFenella'sbaby?* began.

I haven't been looking too good lately. So much, the internship with Carrington, the one I've been hoping to start for two years, fell through.

Again.

My father said it had been a board decision, that they didn't think my image was suitable for a toy company. My image as a party princess, an heiress to the most profitable toy company after Mattel—and that was only after the Barbie movie—and the woman who claimed to be able to tame the baddest boy of rock may not fit the family company, but I do.

I have so many ideas and no one will listen to them.

It didn't help that my twin brother Ashton convinced Dad to sponsor a NASCAR car with Ashton driving, only to have him lose his temper and intentionally bump another car, sending them both spiralling out of the race with only one lap to go.

Dad said it embarrassed the company, which is worse than embarrassing him.

My phone chimes yet again and my twin telepathy has me picking it up.

Ashton: u ok?

Well, that's nice. But he didn't use the group chat so he can keep his grump status intact.

Me: of course

Ashton: you lie

Me: just a little

I can tell Ashton anything, but there's no sense talking about this with him because he made his dislike of Tiger apparent at the very beginning. It had something to do with him dating the ex-girlfriend of Opium's drummer. Or maybe the sister of the guitarist? I can't remember.

I need a wider circle of friends.

I roll over onto my back. My friends ask why I haven't gotten my own place, but when your parents own three homes—four if you count the new villa in Turks and Caicos—and your every need is taken care of when you stay in one of the houses, why would I get my own place?

And I definitely don't want to live with my brother.

My room—a suite of rooms, if you're being particular—was decorated in a sage green back in January because I had gone through a difficult breakup back then and it was better for my spiritual well-being to have a relaxing colour palette.

I think I should change it to hot pink because I am fired up about Tiger.

My phone chimes again before I can pull up my Pinterest décor page. There's no twin telepathy this time, just a general unease because it's my father's ringtone.

Dad: join me for dinner tonight

That's never a good sign.

I don't know if it's good or bad that this isn't a family dinner. It could be about what happened, but it could be because I spoke to Dad again last week about taking a position within the company. I want to show the world I'm not just a cover girl. Plus, I was impressed with Prince Gunnar taking on more princely duties in Laandia.

Prince Gunnar is one of my ex-boyfriends, but the only one who has become one of my best friends. We spent a few weeks together back in February, and I got invited to the royal wedding of his brother Prince Odin and Lady Camille back in June.

I had a mild flirtation with his eldest brother Kalle, the crown prince of Laandia when I was there, but that's neither here nor there.

I like Laandia. After New York and London, and Barcelona and Tokyo, Laandia is one of my favourite places to visit.

It's only my father and me for dinner, as my mother is still at the London house, and Ashton is somewhere in Europe. We talk mainly about Ashton, and I give him the gossip because Dad enjoys that.

I think everything is fine—until it isn't.

"My dear girl, I need you to keep a low profile for the next bit," Dad says, swirling his second glass of Cabernet Sauvignon from our Napa vineyard.

"Has the board said anything?" I demand.

"No, and they won't if you can remove any connection between you and that degenerate singer selling tabloids. It's a conservative board and they will not understand."

I don't understand, I imagine my father saying, but he would never because that would initiate an in-depth conversation about my likes and dislikes, and romantic relationships, and our father-daughter bond doesn't do well with talks like that.

"Do you understand why I was so upset?" No one has asked about the why behind my outburst, which means they already assume Tiger must have cheated or knew and didn't tell me.

"My darling girl, it doesn't matter what I think, or what he did or you did or if neither of you did anything. You are in the public eye, which is your choice since you continue to play around the world."

I'm not sure if *playing* or *partying* sounds better.

"When people see you in that light, you will always be at fault, even when you're innocent of any wrongdoing," he continues in his mild lecturing voice. He never really gets upset with me.

My therapist suggests I have issues with the fact my father never gets upset about anything I do. I'm not sure I agree. My mother seems disappointed in everything, so it's a refreshing change to have one parent on my side.

"I am innocent," I say in a quiet voice.

He pats my hand. "I know, but unfortunately no one else will see you that way. Let's talk about you taking a little vacation. A quiet little vacation."

SILAS

I SET THE PUMPKIN spice latte and warmed cinnamon bun on the counter. "Mrs. Geordie, your order's ready," I call to the older woman.

At least I think she's older—Mrs. Geordie wears more makeup than a circus clown and sports decidedly *young* clothes. Today's combination is a cropped Hello Kitty T-shirt complete with sequins, and ripped jeans so baggy she could fit her dog in there. Said dog is pulling at his leash, salivating at the thought of getting a bite of the cinnamon bun Mrs. Geordie will give him as she gossips about the upcoming royal wedding of Prince Kalle and my cousin, Edie England.

There's enough bun for the both of them; Sweets Ashore, the town bakery that supplies them has been making them bigger and bigger for a while now.

"Nathalia, watch the frother," Leodie says, a note of irritation in her voice.

That note has been there for a while. Three weeks and two days to be exact, ever since I was forced to hire Nathalia because of a lack of anyone else.

I have a good team. Leodie has become one of my best friends, and Jem is a riot to be around with his pop culture genius that has him randomly quoting movie dialogue and song lyrics. Daphne, who used to work here—

But Daphne is gone and I had to find someone else, so Nathalia came aboard. I suspected from the start that it wasn't a good idea, but I was desperate. Having the store open ten hours a day, every day, with only three to staff is a bit much. I'd love to replace Nathalia with two others, but hiring and firing is my least favourite thing to do.

The door opens again, and with it comes a gust of chilly October air. Cheerful fall sweaters and brightly coloured scarves have been the norm around Battle Harbour since early September because when the wind starts coming down from the Arctic, it gets cold around here. Today is one of those days; the bright sun is hidden among ominous gray clouds.

There has been a rumour of snow all morning but I think it's too early. The wind will clear things up and we'll have sun again tomorrow.

At least I hope. We're busier when it's nice out.

I make coffee, warm up pastries. I smile and chat, and wish everyone a nice morning. I do the same thing every day, and I do it well.

Coffee for the Sole might not have been my first love, but it does have a big piece of my heart and I'm happy here.

The door opens again and brings a burst of laughter with it. I don't look up until I hear Leodie's gasp.

An actual gasp, so I check it out.

Prince Gunnar walks in, which is no big surprise, nor is seeing him with Stella Laz, his new girlfriend. Leodie's reaction comes from who is with them: the dark-haired, extremely good-looking man who looks around like my shop is beneath him, and Fenella Carrington.

Fenella Carrington.

I blink and she's still here. Still here and moving closer, close enough for me to take in the drops of rain gleaming like diamonds in her black hair and the way her pink scarf brings out the colour in her cheeks.

"Ash, stop being a Starbucks snob," Fenella says to the dark-haired man as she approaches the counter. "If you want coffee, this is the place to get it."

"Considering we don't have a Starbucks here in Battle Harbour, you'd be out of luck," Stella adds.

"What kind of place doesn't have a Starbucks?" he mutters, and I recognize the etched cheekbones as belonging to Ashton Carrington, Fenella's twin brother.

I'm not sure who catches more of Leodie's attention—her gaze switches from Ashton to Fenella and back again like she's watching a tennis match.

There are two customers between the group and me, and time slows down to a crawl while I serve them.

She's just a girl, I tell myself. *She won't even notice me.*

Why should she? It's Fenella Carrington. *I just saw her very public breakup online.*

And what do I say about that? Sorry about your loss? Nice aim with the ring?

"Hi, Silas," Stella says. "Can I get my regular?"

"Sure thing. The dogs don't need you today?" Stella runs Catch a Pet rescue centre and is single-handedly responsible for the lack of strays in town, cats and dogs both.

Is it my imagination, or do Stella's cheeks turn a becoming shade of pink? Maybe not as becoming as Fenella's scarf reflection, but still attractive. "Ajax is there," she tells me stiffly. "And I've hired a couple more because I'm taking time off—"

Prince Gunnar drops his arm around her shoulders and I swear, most of the women in the shop sigh in unison at the affectionate gesture. "More travelling. We're out of here next week."

"Sounds great." I don't have to ask Gunnar what he wants because he always gets the same—Americano with a shot of hazelnut—but I turn to Ashton Carrington with an expectant smile.

I'm a man content with my appearance, but it's hard not to feel intimidated when faced with Ashton's model-like attractiveness. He's a cross between Timothée Chalamet and the tall guy from Euphoria, and I have no idea how he fits those shoulders into a race car.

"What's good?" he asks brusquely.

"Everything," Fenella answers for me, pushing her way before her brother. "He'll have the same as me—"

"Pumpkin spice latte with two pumps of pumpkin, one of vanilla, oat milk, and unicorn froth," I say.

Fenella's eyes widen with delight, and her purple eyes are so much more striking in person rather than on-screen. "You remembered."

"That's his job," Ashton drawls. "He gets paid to remember."

Ah. A good-looking jerk. But I force a smile at him anyway. "Pumpkin spice is a fall thing but you ordered it in the summer," I say to Fenella. "Hard to forget that."

She beams, and the brightness of her smile is like the sun cresting over the water. "It's my favourite thing in the world."

That smile makes me feel like *I'm* her favourite thing in the world.

"You said that about the dirty martini you had last week," Ashton points out and Fenella scrunches her nose at him, making her model good looks suddenly more human.

There is nothing else down-to-earth about her—she's wearing a shiny pink puffer coat, open to reveal a tight, cream-coloured sweater tucked into wide-legged cream-coloured pants with a faint pink plaid and pristine pink running shoes.

Folks in Battle Harbour don't walk around dressed like that. Normal people anywhere don't walk around like that—or maybe they do. Fenella is the epitome of someone who has 'come from away', which is what we call out-of-towners here in Laandia.

I think I may be paying too much attention if I notice the pink plaid of her pants, but how can you not? Fenella Carrington looks like she stepped off a magazine cover right into my shop.

"I'll get your order started," I tell them.

"Can I get a cinnamon bun as well?" she asks, taking out her phone.

"Sure." Because that's my job. I pour coffee and serve warm pastries for my customers, regardless if they are regulars or first-time tourists, if they have saved their change for a coffee or can buy and sell the entirety of Battle Harbour with their pocket change.

And the fact that Fenella smiled at me with her pretty purple eyes means absolutely nothing.

I watch out of the corner of my eye as she takes pictures of my shop. The pictures on the wall. The glass-fronted display case with the selection of pastries from the bakery.

I put that in after I took over the place from my parents.

Fenella continues to pan around the room, focusing on my brand-new and uber-expensive espresso maker and the float of steam drifting up.

Is that a video, because she's speaking to the screen?

"Enough," her brother finally says. "I thought you didn't want anyone to know where you are?"

"No one will know," Fenella says off-handedly. "Even if I post it, no one will recognize this place. It's so cute, though, isn't it?"

"Sometimes I wonder about your taste," Ashton grumbles.

Fenella elbows him. "My taste for pumpkin spice, you mean?"

Despite Fenella's lightheartedness, their comments don't feel great. Coffee for the Sole might be the first choice for coffee in Battle Harbour, but Battle Harbour is a tiny town on the edge of the Atlantic Ocean. Big fish, small pond and serving Fenella and Ashton Carrington makes me so very aware of that. We're miles away from anything Fenella would consider interesting.

Why should I care about what she considers interesting?

Order in hand, the foursome waves as they take their leave. Leodie is at my side as soon as the door shuts after them. "Did that just happen?" she says excitedly.

"We have royal customers almost every day."

"Not Prince Gunnar—*them*." Stars are shining in her dark eyes. I have seen Leodie's reactions of many things, but I've never seen her starstruck by a model/celebrity influencer, and her good-looking brother.

The Carrington twins are billionaires, but that doesn't make them any different than the rest of us.

I flash back to Fenella's purple eyes; maybe she's a little different. But different isn't always good.

"I heard she's staying at the castle," Leodie tells me excitedly. "Wyatt will blow his mind when he hears. Is he still stalking her online?"

"Who?" I ask, even though I know who she means.

"Fenella Carrington." She gives me a knowing glance. "I saw how she looked at you."

"She's a model. She's paid to look at people like that."

"Nope, there's something there," Leodie insists.

"She needed her morning coffee." I put a hand on the top of Leodie's head. I may not have the Princes of Laandia's height—those boys are tall drinks of water—but I'm a solid six foot and Leodie is pretty short.

She swats my hand away because she hates being reminded of the height difference, which is why I do it. "You're a very silly girl if you think there's ever going to be something there between Fenella and me," I inform her. "That's fairy-tale talk."

"But we live in Laandia and that's better than a fairy tale," she points out.

She does have a point.

Fenella

LAANDIA IS BORING.

It's my third day here and I had no idea hiding out in a foreign country would be so deadly dull.

It's not that dull, but there's nothing to do.

Prince Gunnar Erickson is one of my closest friends and best ex (don't tell him), so when he offered me a safe haven in the castle, it was a no-brainer. It's not like I've never been here—this is my fourth time, plus one of those visits was for Prince Odin's wedding—but Battle Harbour is a small place and I've already checked out everything there is to check out.

We've been to The King's Hat pub twice, gone into every store in what constitutes as a downtown in Battle Harbour. Yesterday, I bundled up in what seemed like every piece of clothing I had and went whale-watching. We had no luck, other than spotting a few seals, and I spent the evening moving from room to room in the castle so I could hug the fireplaces because I was still cold.

Gunnar's new girlfriend Stella insisted we go to the Maritime Museum of Laandia so that I could learn the history of the country—how Battle Harbour was the site of the fight between the Vikings who came to plunder in the 1600s and the bands of First Nations who weren't keen on being pillaged.

The First Nations lost, and the Vikings became the first settlers of what would eventually become the country of Laandia.

In the museum, there's an entire video series about the Second World War, how Leif Erickson prevented the German invasion of Canada, and how grateful the country was for his assistance, that they gave him whatever he wanted, which was his own country.

I thought I was entitled, but even I've never asked for a country before.

Laandia was carved from the province of Newfoundland and Labrador and presented to the family to rule as they liked. King Magnus is the third king and they've done a pretty good job of it.

Learning about the other kings was interesting, but I've never been much for history.

It was better when Ashton was here; at least I wasn't playing third wheel to a deliriously happy Gunnar and Stella. But Ashton left early this morning; Gunnar is flying him to New York and then staying the night with Stella.

I would have liked to go with them but I need to Stay. Out. Of. Sight.

Father's orders.

So now I'm here on my own. Alone.

I'm not used to being alone.

One of the castle security details gives me a ride into Battle Harbour because I've decided I need to get out of the castle. During the drive down the hill (really a cliff with a windy road that wouldn't be out of place heading into the Pyrenees Mountains in Spain) into the town (more like a village) I text the group chat instead of looking out the window at the colourful autumn leaves.

> Me : Day 3 of hiding out.

I send a picture of the view of the harbour outside my bedroom window that I took yesterday.

> Coral: Looks dull

> Me: It's… quiet

> Milo: You're bored. Should we come liven things up?

> Me: I don't think the town has recovered from the last time you were here

> Rupert: That was a good party

> Milo: Didn't Lav end up proposing to a fisherman?

> Lavina: Sweet man, but really couldn't handle this.

She sends a picture, one that should never get on-line—Lavinia wearing a pair of baggy sweats, long blonde hair fixed into two wobbling space buns with one of the facial masks that look like a piece of ham on her face.

> Rupert: not many can

> Me: love you all. Off to shop

> Milo: Where??????

Maybe I will go shopping, but we hit all four clothing shops the day before yesterday, which leaves the bookstore, the bakery and a return visit to the candy store.

I could do with a visit to the candy store.

I get out of the car in the centre of town. There's a cool wind blowing in off the harbour but the afternoon sun is warm and bright. It really is a pretty place.

But boring.

Maybe boring isn't the right word. Quiet. Uneventful. What's another word for "there is nothing to do"?

There are five bars; I know this because the second time I visited, Gunnar and I did a bar hop and visited all of them. That was before Gunnar was Gunnar-and-Stella so there was still the undercurrent of flirtation, even though we had been broken up for years.

Not that there was any chance of us getting back together. Once you break up, that's it for me, sexy prince or no sexy prince.

Tiger is out of luck.

My first stop before my walkabout is Coffee for the Sole.

The heady aroma of coffee greets me, along with the chatter of customers waiting in line or seated at the tables. Two of the leather armchairs are empty by the window, which would be perfect to curl up in, but sit in a coffee shop by myself? That's something I would do with Lavinia or Rupert. This whole alone thing will take more than a minute to get used to.

The hum of the coffee machine breaks over the background music as I take my place in line. Every single person I make eye contact with—and the place is pretty full—smiles at me.

That will also take some getting used to.

It's unnerving, but they're not the smiles of recognition, just pleasant, polite people saying good afternoon. I'm sure it's a small-town thing, but I can't be sure.

Behind the counter, Silas moves with an ease that suggests he's been doing this for a while. He's got a geek/boy-next-door vibe going on, and the flannel shirts make him seem outdoorsy. The whole package is not really my thing, but he's certainly nice to look at. Tall and shaggy with hair that needs a cut and some product to put it in place, and green eyes that always look like he needs a nap.

Something certainly keeps that boy up at night.

He-who-is-cute runs his hand through his hair, tousling it like he just woke up and grins at the short girl behind the counter with him. His whole face lights up like she's the most important person in the world.

I want him to look at me like that.

And I shouldn't. Why should I want that?

It's been a week since my discovery that Tiger was a lying, cheating jerk. He sent me sixty-seven texts, full of explanations and remorse, but no real apology. I blocked his number, and unfollowed him on social media—the usual stuff.

Tiger told TMZ that he didn't understand the exclusivity restraints of our relationship. You give a girl a ring; that means you're exclusive.

He was in it for the publicity. I know that now.

I'd know it even if everyone didn't tell me that fact.

Being seen with me can boost a fading career, or jumpstart a new one. I once made Rickie Fowler the darling of the PGA tour for six weeks, showing up at three tournaments and causing fourteen people to be escorted off the green. I don't know if it was me as his good luck charm, or if he just decided to step up his game, but Rickie made it to the Masters that year. He didn't win the Green Jacket, but it doesn't matter because we broke up before the tournament.

Even bad publicity is good, and Opium holds three of the top ten songs on Spotify and Apple Music this week.

Yes, I checked. I didn't want to but it had to be done.

And Tiger is making the most of it—appearing everywhere he can to promote the group and himself as the wounded boyfriend.

He cheated on *me*.

That seems to be forgotten in his narrative. Yesterday, Coral sent me the video of Tiger's heartfelt plea for me to forgive him for whatever I think he's done.

No comment from me, because...really?

Plus, my father gave me stern instructions not to engage with the press while I'm here. It was nice enough of Gunnar to offer me safe haven in Laandia, and amazingly kind of King Magnus to issue a four-week ban on any outside press entering the country.

It's not the first time I've picked the wrong guy. Usually, I jump straight to the next mistake while the reels are still viral, but for some reason, I'm not jumping this time. There's been a long list of men I've dated; men who treat me like a princess in public, and the lowly pea under the mattress in private. Men who want one thing from me—instant fame and to rub against my bank account. Men, who don't care about *me*.

Because of this, I know I wouldn't have the faintest idea of what to do with a nice guy.

Silas seems like a nice guy, with his flannels and his scruff and kind eyes.

I focus on the rest of the coffee shop instead of wondering if the beard is usual or just because he's forgotten to shave. He's very easy to look at but so is the rest of the place. I'd say eclectic, really going for the small-town fishing vibe with nets and buoys and pictures of boats. The walls are dark blue and decorated with vintage signs advertising coffee and cream and cans of tuna, alongside framed art prints and canvases, and crayon-coloured pictures.

I like the one with the barista holding a huge to-go cup that's bigger than his head.

There's also a fish—it's animated and the head and tail flop as a song is played.

It's interesting. It might not be my first choice, but there's no other choice. There's no Starbucks, no Cha Cha Matcha, or not even the Canadian favourite, Tim Horton's. Gunnar told me Laandia refuses to allow franchises in the country.

There's not even a McDonalds here.

It's like one of those little Italian villages that serve dinner out of the back of someone's house.

It's not as slow moving though; the line jumps quickly to my turn. It's not Silas—sad—or the short girl, but a woman with brassy blonde hair from a bad dye job and heavy eyeliner that makes her look about ten years older than I imagine she is.

She also looks even more bored than I am, constantly checking her phone on the counter beside her.

That all changes when I give my name and she does the most dramatic double-take I've ever seen, even counting the time I walked around Soho in a bralette. "You're Fenella Carrington?" she practically shrieks.

"No," I say automatically, taking a step back.

Already, I imagine phones are out, filming, taking pictures. Telling the world where I am. "No, I'm not." I usually give a fake name at Starbucks since there aren't many Fenellas who order pumpkin spice throughout the year. There aren't many Fenellas, period.

Thanks to my grandmother for my so very unique name.

"You are?" Everything about the woman is wide open—eyes, mouth. Even her nostrils are flaring. Her name tag says *Nathalia*, and I really wish Nathalia weren't working today.

"Are you telling me or asking?" I demand.

"I'm...telling."

"I know my own name, thank you very much."

She frowns. "You are, aren't you?" I look over but Silas has disappeared. Not that I looked to him to rescue me but—

Okay, maybe a little rescue. He looks like the rescuing type. "Now you're asking," I say coolly. "Can I have my drink?"

Nathalia blinks, mouth still open. She seems a little older than my usual fan, more like one of the conservative Karens who criticize every step of my life. The incorrect use of bronzer and unshaped brows also suggests she doesn't follow old makeup tutorials. "What did you want again?" she asks. "I was distracted."

"Pumpkin spice latte, with two pumps and an extra of vanilla, oat milk, unicorn froth."

Granted, a latte isn't a simple drink but it's one of those with a three-inch order attached. But where I stand gives me a perfect vantage point to watch her totally mess up my drink.

Three pumps, so that's going to be really pumpkin-y.

"Vanilla," I remind her as she gives a pump of caramel. "And oat milk."

"You said almond," Nathalia says as she pours almond milk into the frother jug.

"No, I said oat."

"Are you allergic?"

I want to say yes. "I don't like almond milk."

She holds it under the steamer spout. "But if you're not allergic, it doesn't matter. Try it this way, you'll like it. In fact, you can make this *the* drink of the fall... I'll give you a drizzle of caramel over the foam—oh, and maybe I'll add a shot of peppermint. No, lavender."

"No thank you." But it doesn't matter—she adds two vigorous pumps. "I'm not drinking that," I declare.

"You have to. I made you a custom drink. You have to try and I'll video—"

She clearly knows nothing about keeping a low profile. "No."

"What do you mean, no? Do it for Silas."

Who is this person? She presents me with the cup with a flourish. "Try it. Love it, and I'll film you."

Nathalia isn't going to like what I have to say. But as I'm revving up, she gets called away by the irritated short girl.

And then Silas appears. "Uh—hi," he greets me. Today's flannel is black and blue, the sleeves rolled up to show strong forearms with a faint dusting of reddish hair.

I pull my gaze away from those arms. "Your employee just made me a drink I didn't order."

There's no masking the expression of resignation and he doesn't even ask who I'm talking about. "What did she make?"

"I have no idea but there's lavender and caramel in this." I give a sniff and grimace. "I would never want lavender in a latte. I ordered a pumpkin spice latte with vanilla."

"I'll make you another. I'm sorry about Nathalia. She—"

"Shouldn't be working here if she can't take a simple order."

There's no one waiting in line after me, and the bustle of the shop seems to have relaxed. Or maybe it's just Silas who is relaxed.

Distressed, but still relaxed. He sighs. "It's not that simple. I really needed to cover shifts and I felt bad—she's my parents' neighbours' daughter, and just got divorced—"

"That's a *her* problem, not a *you* problem."

Silas frowns. "I'm helping her out and—"

"Does she need the money?"

He glances over his shoulder to where the short girl is gesturing to the jug of steamed milk that has been left on the counter. "I don't think so."

"Then there's no reason for her to work here if she's incompetent." A voice rises—something about beans—and I look at Silas expectantly.

"I know." He lowers his voice. "I haven't been able to bring myself to tell her." He shrugs with a sheepish smile.

Huh. I didn't expect this. He's...huh.

Maybe I should revisit nice guys. Especially ones from Laandia.

"Of course I'm right." I cock my head. "Are you..." I drop my voice. "A *nice* guy?"

"What?"

"You can't fire her because you're too nice."

"That's not... maybe? Is that bad?" He gives me a smile that is half confused, half apologetic, and all the way adorable.

Oh no. My stomach flips at the sight of his smile. Slightly crooked, teeth not perfect but wow, that dimple is deep enough for me to stick my finger in it. The whole package is making *me* smile.

"It's rare. I only know a few of the species." I give him my camera-ready smile and his eyes glaze over for a moment. "Because of that, I'm going to help you out."

SILAS

I DON'T UNDERSTAND WHAT'S going on, probably because I seem to be blinded by Fenella.

Snow-blinded, maybe. She's wearing all white today—pants tight at the hips with twin rows of buttons running diagonally to her waist and a loose sweater cropped at her belly button. Her coat might be denim and falls just below her knees.

How much luggage did she bring?

I watched her through the tiny window in the back storage room when she was ordering and I could tell Nathalia was making her the wrong drink but couldn't bring myself to intervene.

Nathalia has only been working here for a little over a week, but I'm already exhausted from telling her what she's doing wrong.

Earlier today, she dropped a bag of our most expensive beans and all she could say was a giggly *oops* as they skittered all over the floor.

Nathalia is almost forty; there should be no giggling over mistakes at that age. At any age. But it was worse when she overboiled the milk because she was checking her phone and decided to argue with Leodie over what she did wrong.

She's a horrible barista. I have to fire her but I hate firing people. It's like my pet peeve and my worst nightmare all rolled into one.

But I don't understand how Fenella can help with that.

"She made me the wrong drink," she says in a loud voice that's about two shades more pretentious than her usual to ne. "And when I corrected her, she insisted I try it, that I could make it a popular drink. She's trying to take advantage of my celebrity when all I wanted when I came here was peace and quiet. Is that too much to ask for?"

I watch as Nancy Tanker and Bernie Carols lower their phones with guilty expressions. Were they filming Fenella? Were they taking *videos* of her? Who does that?

"Your coffee shop is suffering with her working here," Fenella announces loud enough for everyone in said coffee shop to hear.

Leodie and Nathalia stop their argument.

Well, she's not wrong. Still—what is she doing? One minute, she seemed fine with the wrong drink and now...

"I'm so sorry," I mutter. "I'll make you another one."

"I don't want another one. I want the one she was supposed to make. If you don't have employees who treat their customers with the respect they deserve, I don't think I want anything from here." She gives me a wink.

Oh, is this... is she only pretending? "I am very sorry that she upset you," I say, raising my voice.

"You should be upset. In fact, you should be so upset that you don't want her to work here any longer."

"What?" Nathalia screeches.

"Caramel is not vanilla," Fenella tells her. "They don't even smell remotely the same. And lavender should not be a part of that drink."

"It's *lavender.* Maybe you should drink it and calm down. Stop the temper tantrums."

The whole place goes silent. Fenella lifts one carefully groomed eyebrow and stares at Nathalia, who pales when she realizes what she said. "I mean, I couldn't tell what I put in because of the overpowering stench of coffee," she protests weakly.

"That's because you dropped the bag of beans earlier and the whole place smells more than it usually does," Leodie points out.

"Which I told you, is not my fault. I had butter on my hands from that croissant I warmed up and—"

"Nathalia," I chide. "We don't argue."

I sound like I'm talking to my nephew. When he was five.

"We do when they're *wrong.* She's trying to get you to fire me because she's famous, Silas—"

"She won't have to try very hard," Leodie mutters.

Fenella crosses her arms and gazes down her nose at Nathalia. With her lips pressed tight together and her purple eyes looking almost black, I suspect Fenella resembles her father on a bad day rather than the model/influencer/partygirl that she is. "I'd be trying to fire you even if I was a nobody like you," she says, her voice as icy as a January wind.

"Nathalia," I begin, unsure of how exactly to do this. Fenella has given me the opening and now I have to take it and run.

"You are *not* taking her side." Nathalia looks incredulous and I half expect her to stomp her foot.

"That's what we do when she's right," Leodie points out like she practiced this with Fenella.

"You're trying to fire me!" By now, every eye in the place is watching and I notice Fenella drift back a foot to get out of range of anyone who may be videoing the exchange. Not that anyone would—

Okay, so Nancy Tanker has her phone trained on Nathalia with an expression of delight on her face. "Nathalia," I try again.

"Oh, no you don't! You're not firing me—I quit!" She rips off her Coffee for the Sole apron with the little fish and thrusts it at me. "I don't need a boss who won't back me up. You're no better than my husband. He refused to take my side over his mother's and I *will not have it.* I won't work for you again, Silas, even if you begged me to." Nathalia grabs her phone that's still on the counter, reaches down and hauls out her coat and purse, when I have explained at least six times that we don't keep personal property out here. "I'm never coming back to work here. Not even if you beg me to."

She waits a beat, like she's actually expecting me to ask her to stay. I don't say a word and she storms out.

The door slowly closes, but it seems that's not enough for Nathalia because she pushes it shut with an angry expression.

"And you will never, ever, beg her for anything, let alone to work here again," Leodie says under her breath.

"I really think she thought you were going to," Fenella comments in her regular tone.

I gesture at Nancy, who is now laughing at the scene. "You should get rid of that," I reprimand, gesturing to her phone. "No one needs to see it." And then I stare out the window where I can see Nathalia stomping across the street. I still have her apron in my hand. "She just quit."

"You're welcome." Fenella flips her black hair behind her shoulder.

I turn to her. "I didn't want her to quit." That's not exactly true, but I definitely don't want to start over trying to find someone who wants to work here. At least I didn't have to look very hard with Nathalia—she asked me for a job, and after working thirteen double shifts without a break, I was desperate enough to agree.

I didn't think working here was that difficult, but she never really got the hang of things. Or really wanted to. But still, the thought of having to start again is not a pleasant one.

"Well, you didn't want to fire her either, so again, you're welcome." Fenella smiles but there's a coolness in her gaze. "That woman was not meant to work here."

"Says... you?"

"Says me, too." Leodie leans over the counter, fist outstretched for Fenella to bump.

"I'm not sure you realize this, but *I'm* in charge here?"

Leodie waves. "You think that, Silas, but... no." She grins conspiratorially at Fenella who... laughs.

Fenella Carrington laughs and it's not a pretty sound. It's almost like she hasn't laughed in a few years and is only now remembering she's able to do so. And the thought of *that* snuffs my annoyance like birthday candles being blown out.

"It will be a more harmonious work environment without Nathalia," Leodie continues. "She was really bringing the moral down."

"You could have told me that earlier rather than stand there and watch her walk out," I say, resigned. "That didn't make anyone look good. And I know she only wanted the job to keep her from being bored during the day, but what if she really needed it? What if she needed the money?" I look at Fenella.

You don't know anything about that. Even though I don't say the words, I can tell the realization hits Fenella. I won't make a judgement about her because I told Leodie the truth—I really don't know her. I know she's a beautiful woman and that, along with her family's fortune has opened doors and given her opportunities that not everyone can have.

It's hard to say if she understands this.

I'm sure she has to deal with a lot—billionaires do have their problems—but they're not the issues that regular people face.

It's clear Fenella Carrington is not a regular person.

And that thought makes me sad.

"Had to be done, Silas," Nancy calls from the table where she and Bernie don't even pretend that they're not listening. "Fenella's right—she had no business working here. You have to respect the bean," she says dramatically. "Nathalia didn't respect the bean."

She's right. They're all right. I shouldn't have hired Nathalia but still... "Do you respect the bean?" I ask Nancy. "Want a job here?"

"No way," Nancy says with a laugh. "I don't even like making coffee for my husband."

I shrug and turn to Leodie. "I liked watching her walk out," she admits. "You should thank Fenella for getting it done because I don't think you could have done it."

"He's too nice a guy," Fenella agrees.

"That doesn't sound like a compliment."

Fenella holds my gaze. "Oh, it is." Up close, her eyes look like they have at least three different shades of purple, but that could be the light. They're almond-shaped and set wide apart in her face, and I can't seem to turn away. "I think I like nice guys."

Fenella is not a regular person and I should kick myself for thinking the thoughts I'm thinking about her. Like how her upper lip is a little fuller than her lower and both turn down at the corners. How her ear is like a delicate shell peeking out from her curtain of dark hair, adorned with diamond studs the size of the nail on my pinkie finger. And how her throat moves as she swallows.

The moment stretches between us and Leodie moves away to serve Andy Babbit, come for his daily chai tea latte on his way home from work.

"You're not sure?" I finally ask.

"I haven't known too many of them," she admits.

"Gunnar is a nice guy." Mentioning an old boyfriend—what am I doing?

"He's a prince. And I'm not princess material."

"I don't know about that."

Fenella's face lights up at that. It's like there's a glow emanating from behind her, illuminating her every feature and making her simply breathtaking.

Seriously. Seeing a happy Fenella takes my breath away.

There's a smile on her face—at least there is until she takes a sip of her drink and winces. "Ew."

I laugh because me just standing here staring at her like she's bewitched me is getting old. "I'm sorry."

"There's nothing for you to be sorry about. That just shows that the person who thought the combo was a good idea has no business working here. Pumpkin, caramel and lavender? No, thank you."

"Let me make you a new one," I offer. "It's the least I can do after you got rid of my employee."

I reach for her cup and my finger brushes against hers.

Is there a spark when I touch her? I can't tell because the scent of cinnamon and cloves drowns out my other senses. Nathalia must have used half the bottle of syrup and I make a mental note to fill it up before the late-afternoon rush starts.

It is better not to have to cleanup after Nathalia, and maybe I'll be able to find someone quickly. It's not like I have anything that gets in the way of doing double shifts. Or anyone. Work, Wyatt, and trying to find time for a regular stargaze sees to that. Neptune will be visible this week and I'd like to get out to the spot near the lighthouse at least once to see it.

"I'm sorry if I crossed a line."

I glance at Fenella. I get the sense she's not the type who apologizes.

Ever.

"You were right," I concede. "I've never had to fire anyone. They just leave by mutual agreement."

"Sounds like this is a good place to work then, you being a nice guy and all." She smiles and this one isn't blinding but natural. And kind of sweet. "Did that sound more like a compliment?"

I hand over her new drink. "Guess so."

And then with a wiggle of her fingers, she's gone.

Fenella

I HAVEN'T GOTTEN SOMEONE fired in a while.

I have gotten people fired before. I'm not proud of it but I like to think they were like Nathalia and not suited for their positions.

I've never once considered they might need the job.

And I don't like that Silas seems to know that.

Demanding Fenella isn't someone I aspire to be; I'm accustomed to the best money can buy, but when I hear that tone in my voice that suggests I'm telling others that I'm better than them, I do my best to turn it off because that's my mother talking.

Adelaide Carrington slipped into my father's orbit with intention because she worked for the company. She started as an intern, moved up to assistant to his office manager. The legend is that they met over coffee—she offered, he refused and made her a cup of tea, the worst she ever tasted. They were married six weeks later.

Less than a year later, my older brother Evan was born, but it was ten years later before Ashton and I were born, me first with him racing out two minutes later.

It's difficult to imagine my parents so caught up into each other that they could only wait such a short time before starting their lives together. I was about ten before I realized they didn't seem that happy with each other.

These days I don't see much of my mother, who prefers whatever house Ashton and I aren't staying at. Evan is her golden child, the pride and joy of the Carrington family and I do my best to ignore my mother as much as she ignores me.

If Nathalia had served her, she would have caused such a big scene that I cringe just thinking about it.

So I don't. I finish my pumpkin spice latte—so delicious the way Silas makes them—and put the whole episode out of my mind.

Taking my new and improved latte, I wander around the downtown streets of Battle Harbour.

Fall has arrived in the little town.

It's a cute little town even without the autumn decorations; containers of red and orange asters outside every shop door, with tiny pumpkins nestled throughout the flowers. Paper cutouts of pumpkins and black cats and colourful leaves stuck to shop windows remind me that Halloween is a little more than a week away.

Instead of a main street, the shopping district—if it can be called that—is a square, with Coffee for the Sole at one corner and The King's Hat pub on the opposite side. A statue of some Erickson Viking ancestor looms in the middle of the space, and cobblestones would make it difficult to cross in some of my thin-heeled shoes.

It's picturesque. And quiet.

Almost too quiet.

It's October, but it feels colder as the sun goes down. I thought I brought warm enough clothes but maybe I need more. For once, the thought of shopping doesn't fill me with the excitement that it usually does.

I stop in at the bookstore and the candy store to waste time. I pause at the window of the flower shop but don't go in because who am I going to buy flowers for?

But I go into the fish and chip place because I see Sophie Laz in the window and we got friendly the last time I was in town. She brings me a piece of fish and half an order of chips and takes her break as I eat.

The restaurant is small and cozy, like most of the businesses in Battle Harbour, with only a few tables. I suspect they do more takeout than fine dining. It's decorated with the same sea motifs as Coffee for the Sole but darker and smells of fish rather than coffee beans.

I take a few pictures even though the lighting is horrible, posing with Sophie and promise to tag her.

"Aren't you bored here?" she demands. "Your life is so fabulous and this place is..."

"Not so fabulous?" I glance around. "It's okay. It's a nice break." I care too much about Gunnar to ever badmouth his country.

Besides, I do like it here. It's just... quieter than what I'm used to.

"What would you be doing if you were home?"

Tonight was Tuesday—Rupert had made reservations at the new vegan fusion restaurant for us, along with Coral and her latest guy. Tomorrow night was the premier of the latest Channing Tatum movie and I had the best outfit to wear.

I should be meeting Ashton in New York on Saturday, and then flying somewhere in the Midwest to see Tiger.

I can strike him out of all my plans. Cancel him completely from my schedule.

"What do you usually spend your time doing?" Sophie asks when I'm too depressed to tell her what I had planned. "When you're at home."

No one has ever asked me that question. Maybe because my friends do the same things I do. "When I'm not on a shoot or doing videos, I... shop. There's yoga and Pilates and Cross Fit, but I got bored with that. And... friends... we go for lunch and... Not much," I finish, looking at my day's activities with a new lens. "I don't do a lot."

"Sounds great," Sophie bubbles.

Is it? Is it great? I want to do more, but no one seems to give me a chance. No one thinks enough of me to let me try.

"Is there a car rental place around here?" I ask Sophie. I'm used to having a driver and a car at my disposal, but there's something about being here alone and having to ask someone at the castle to come and get me that irks me.

"The big one is by the airport, but over on Fourth Street, they have a lot where they rent out vans and pickup trucks for things. Are you going somewhere?" Sophie is sweet and cute and a little too excited about my life, but it's okay. It has to be okay because I really have no one else in town.

I could do a pickup truck. My brother may be the race car driver, but I learned to drive alongside him, and there's nothing I can't tackle. "Back and forth to Hotel Castle. I'd rather come and go on my own schedule than rely on pickups and drop-offs. I notice you don't have Ubers around here." I take a bite of my fish—some kind of white fish, draped in a thick batter with grease staining the wax paper lining the basket. It smells amazing and tastes even better.

The only fish I've been eating lately is sushi. This is definitely not sushi.

"I can't believe you're staying there like it's a hotel." Sophie sighs like my travel arrangements make up some kind of fairy tale.

"Doesn't your dad live there?" I'm not sure what his exact title is, but if this were Washington, Duncan Laz would be Chief of Staff, Secretary of State, and VP combined. I've met him a few times, and he's incredibly attractive for an older man. He doesn't have the charisma of King Magnus, but in my opinion, Duncan is better-looking.

I'm not about to tell that to his daughter though.

"Yes, but I don't," Sophie says. "Stella practically does though with Gunnar when they're in town."

Stella, Prince Gunnar's new girlfriend, is Sophie's sister. I like to think I had a hand in them getting together during my earlier visit.

"They're cute together." And they are. I've never stayed on good terms with any of my other ex-boyfriends, but my friendship with Gunnar has lasted longer than our relationship and I value it a lot more. It's easy to be happy for him because of that.

There is no way I will be staying on good terms with Tiger.

It's annoying how he floats into my mind at random moments, like a falling leaf. Leaves in October are colourful and beautiful but essentially dead as soon as they disconnect from the tree, and that's what I consider Tiger. He's dead to me.

"Does it bother you?" Sophie wants to know. I push the basket toward her and she takes a French fry. One piece of fish is huge and there's no way I'm going to be able to finish this order. Although, my appetite seems to be growing since I've come here. Maybe it's something about the sea air.

I take another bite of fish before I answer. "No. I was over Gunnar before we broke up."

"Really? I always thought you and him..."

"It was good while we were together, but it was years ago. We were different people. All he wanted to do was race cars and I wanted to be with my friends."

"I'm surprised no one is here with you. Your brother—"

"Ashton can only take the quiet life for so long. He needs to be constantly moving."

"He's really cute."

"I'll tell him you said so."

"No, don't." She giggles and I laugh because she seems so much younger than me.

Sophie goes back to work and I finish my meal alone, watching the steady line of customers come to pick up their dinners.

I picture them taking their fish and chips home to their families—middle-aged women, fishermen weathered and tan from being on the ocean for days at a time, and one little boy who runs in to pick up three bags of food. Sophie talks to him for a few minutes and walks him to the door.

It's all very homey.

I'm not sure I can get used to that.

Silas crosses my mind, and I wonder about his home. I've never seen him outside the coffee shop but he can't be selling coffee all the time.

Unlike my floating thoughts about Tiger and our breakups, thinking about Silas doesn't annoy me. At all.

The man is attractive. There's no denying that—tall, broad, and green-eyed with no visible tattoos, exactly what I need

after the debacle with Tiger. But something about him tells me
to stay away. Far away.

I'm not sure if it's because Silas seems like a genuinely nice
guy or if behind the cheerful grin, I get the sense there is some
hidden baggage.

I could be imagining things, or else the baggage I sense is
mine.

Either way, I won't be around here long enough to find out
for sure.

But in the meantime, I need to see someone about a car.

Sophie was right; there is a car rental place, if that's what
you can call a building lot full of cars, most of them trucks.
I've been waiting here for ten minutes and no one is around. I
even knocked on the front door of the house next to it but no
answer.

No car for me. I glance down the street; it's about five blocks
away from the centre of Battle Harbour and the homes seem
to get more rundown the further away I walk. I should go back
to where I came from and call for a ride because I have no idea
of street names around here.

Something tells me to keep walking.

There are no sidewalks, and fallen leaves are piled up on the side of the road. I kick through them, enjoying the crunchy sound, until the toe of my boot hits something solid.

Then I walk in the middle of the road.

Five minutes later, I see it—the unmistakable silhouette of a Dodge Charger parked on the lawn of a tired home.

It's yellow.

And I see the For Sale sign in the window.

I skirt around the car, running my hand along the lines of the hood, feeling more excited than I have in a long time. My father designed a series of model cars based on real-life vehicles and the muscle cars were always my favourite. Ashton has always been drawn to pure speed, but I like the roar and the rumble and the feel of power at my fingertips.

"Help you out?"

I look up with surprise, so fixated on the car that I didn't notice the man walking toward me. "You're from away," he says. It's not a question and I recognize the wariness of locals when they first talk to me.

Although, I've never talked to locals who look like him—tanned and leathery and very wrinkled, like he's gone years without using sunscreen.

"If that means I'm not from around here, then yes. I want to buy your car." There's no reason for small talk.

He makes a noise that may be a laugh or might be phlegm caught in his throat. "Nobody wants that car."

"I do."

"You trying to tell me you want the car just because of the pretty colour?"

"I'm not trying to tell you anything. I'm telling you that I'm interested in this car."

"That's a lot of car for a lass like you," he says scornfully.

"It's a 2007? Or a 2008? Dodge Charger SRT8 with a Hemi engine. V-8. Looks in good shape." I give the tire a kick. "Except for the dirt." The bright yellow paint is covered by a thin layer of dust.

"2007," he says. "Are you sure you can handle this much car?"

"Do you know who I am?"

He shrugs. "Should I? I'm Coy Schmidt. Most folks in town know who I am. If you want it, lass, you best have a look." He pops the hood and I bend over it eagerly.

The engine was just as I described and, already, I can imagine the rumbly throb. I ask the right questions and give the right answers because Coy disappears into the house to grab the keys while I climb into the driver's seat.

The inside is pristine, the leather soft and dark brown, and smelling of cleaning product. "Cleaned it just last weekend but the crap in the trees made a mess of the outside," he complains as he opens the passenger door.

"You mean leaves?"

"That and the other." I have no idea what else is falling from the trees and Coy's accent is so thick that it's hard to understand him. But I understand completely when he hands me the keys. "Let's see what you can do with it," he says.

I can't stop the grin that spreads across my face as I start it up.

The entire car vibrates. "Why are you selling this?" I marvel as I grip the gearshift.

"The wife hates it. I spend my days on the boat, and she says I'm not to spend my nights driving around in my fancy car looking to pick up women."

I glance over with surprise. "Do you pick up many women in this car?"

Coy *pshaws*. "No."

I'm not about to get in the middle of this when all I want to do is try this baby out. "Hang on," I warn.

"Now, just a sec here," Coy sputters as I rev the engine. The car practically leaps like it's bursting from the starting blocks, leaving tire marks amid the mud and wet leaves.

"Zero to sixty in less than six seconds," I cry, giving a whoop of delight. Coy grabs the doorhandle.

I've always loved driving, always been fascinated with cars. When I was five years old, I demanded the latest cars the company was making, same as Ashton, and it was my idea for Dad to commission the real live models of his most popular toy cars. I made his driver teach me the basics of car repair, not that I've ever needed to do it myself.

I don't even own a car at home; it's too easy to take my pick of my father's stable of high-end vehicles when I want to drive.

I've never wanted to race cars like Ashton does, but whenever I could, I'd show up in the middle of his pit crew and take in as much as I could as I cheered my brother on.

I take the corner too fast and speed up as I straighten out.

I could buy this car.

I don't go far, just around the neighbourhood, with Coy pointing out different houses and describing problems he's had with the people who live there.

"You seem like a popular guy," I tell him as I pull back into the drive.

"Well, yeah," he says. "If you want the car, you best come into the house. The wife's getting supper ready." He gets out without waiting for a reply.

It's one thing to have him in the car with me when I'm doing the driving, but I'm too much of a city girl not to feel more than a hint of uncertainty at the thought of going into his house.

His wife is home.

How do I ever know there's actually a wife? He could have made her up.

But still, I follow him to the side door, telling myself not to make this into a big deal. And when he holds the door open, I'm happy to see the figure of a woman in the kitchen.

The inside is more appealing than the outside. Warm and tidy with framed pictures on every surface. There's Coy at different stages of his life, never with a smile. The woman beside him more than makes up for it.

I shiver—the warmth of the home makes me realize how cold I was.

Coy nods at the woman at the stove. To her credit, there's no surprise in her expression at the sight of me with her husband, only the usual mild wariness. "That's Laura," he says to me. "Pet, she wants to buy the car."

Laura throws up her hands, one still holding a wooden spoon and a few drops splatter over the floor. "Thank the Jesus for that. But it's too big a car for a lass like her," she warns.

"D'yu know who she is?" Coy asks his wife as if I'm not standing there. "She asks me but I've no idea."

"She stays at the castle, a friend of the Gunny Prince," Laura reports without a second glance at me. "Famous for something, I hear. You in the movies, lass?"

This is the part that always stings. I'm famous for being famous, like the Kardashians before their makeup empire took over the world. Like Paris Hilton, back in the day. Hailey Bieber. I'm famous because of my father, or to be blunt, because of my father's money.

I've always been accused of doing nothing to earn my celebrity. The echo of it sticks in, like a thorn piercing the soft skin of my hand every time I try to smell a rose.

Of course I'm not about to admit this to anyone, let alone a grumpy fisherman and his wife. "You might have seen me in magazines," I tell Laura.

"A model? Huh. Guess that explains why you're so gosh darn skinny. Best pull up a chair for some chowder. It's going to be a chilly one and you look cold."

I can't argue with that.

I sit at the table with Coy and Laura and accept a steaming bowl of fish chowder and a glass of milk. They ask a few questions about Gunnar and King Magnus, but mainly I listen to their conversation as I finish every mouthful.

Laura pours me a second glass of milk when I tell her I don't remember the last time I had a glass of it.

Twenty minutes after I finish, I send a text to the group chat.

Me: I bought a car!

SILAS

I'VE JUST FINISHED CLEANING the coffee maker when there's a bang on the locked door.

Wyatt.

My nephew at sixteen is already my height and might someday out-broad my shoulders if he keeps growing like he has been. "You're late," I pretend to grouse as I let him in. "I saved all the dirty jobs for you."

"You do know I don't work here during the week, right?" He grins, and like always, it's a bittersweet sight. I love that Wyatt is such a good-tempered, great-natured kid, but when he smiles, he looks exactly like my sister Emily.

And even after sixteen years, it still hurts that she left us. Left Wyatt. Left me, her little brother and best friend, or so she always said.

Because my parents were convinced they did something wrong in raising my sister, they have enrolled Wyatt in every activity that is offered in Battle Harbour. And to our amazement, Wyatt showed an aptitude for most of them. He's the star third baseman of the Harbour Howlers under-eighteen team, designed a comic book, and plays guitar. He's good at school, focusing on science.

He likes astronomy.

I started teaching him about the stars when he was in kindergarten, taking him to the lighthouse up the coast when there was something special to see.

It's our thing now.

Working double shifts at the coffee shop means I haven't had much time lately to go star gazing with Wyatt, but I need to go tonight. Neptune should be in sight, plus the Draconid meteor shower begins in less than two weeks. There's nothing I want more than to check out the night sky with my nephew.

"What's Fenella Carrington doing in town?" Wyatt demands as I finish behind the counter.

"How do you even know who she is?" I wonder.

"Dude. Over seventeen million followers, plus that Michael Kors campaign last year where she's wearing *just* the handbag? Please tell me you've seen that."

"Please tell me why *you've* seen it?"

"Uncle Silas," Wyatt says in a girlish voice. "I'm a homosexual, not an idiot. I can appreciate the beauty of a woman as much as a man." He cocks his head, longish dark hair falling to the side. "But the important question is: do you appreciate that woman's beauty?"

"What exactly are you asking?" I pick up the to-go cups—my vanilla latte and a hot chocolate for Wyatt—as I motion Wyatt to the back door.

"I heard she's been in here a lot. Did you ask her out?"

I laugh. "Why would I do that?"

He throws up his hands. "Why would you—dude. It's Fenella Carrington. Naked with a handbag. She's *hot*, Silas, and you could use some of that in your life."

"I definitely do not need some Fenella Carrington in my life."

"Can I meet her?"

"I'm not about to introduce you to her. She'll be gone in a few days anyway and your hormones can go back to normal. Or whatever has got you so excited."

"She's very attractive," Wyatt reminds me as I lock the back door and head to my car parked in the tiny space off the alley.

"I agree, but I don't go around asking out every attractive woman."

"You should. It's been a long time since you've been on a date. Hey, can I drive?"

"No, it'll be dark before we get there and you're not allowed to drive after dark."

"I'm not allowed to drive anywhere," he grumbles as he slides in the passenger side.

"No, you're not. I'll take you out next week," I promise as I start the car. "When you're done studying for that English test."

"Technically, it's very difficult to study for an English test," Wyatt informs me as I maneuver down the alley to First Street. "You just keep reading over and over again."

"Then read over and over again and when I decide it's enough, I'll take you driving."

Wyatt came into my world when I was fourteen and he disrupted everything. I spent the first six weeks of his life furious with my sister for bringing him home—I was an innocent fourteen and I didn't dwell on how exactly my seventeen-year-old sister ended up with a baby in the first place—until my mother stuck Wyatt in my arms one night when he wouldn't stop crying.

He stopped for me; for a few glorious moments, our house was quiet as Wyatt's big blue eyes tried to focus on my face.

And then he took the biggest poo of his young life, all the way up his diaper, soaking through his sleeper and onto my T-shirt. I didn't care; in those few moments where Wyatt stared at me, a bond was forged and I pledged my life to my baby nephew.

Sixteen years later, Wyatt is still a huge part of my life.

"So when's the last time you had a date?" Wyatt asks as I take the coast road out of town.

"Why are we talking about *my* dating life when it's you who wants to invite Brody to the Halloween party? How's that going?"

"Done. There's no point stressing about it—I like him, I asked him, and he said yes."

There's not a large LGBTQ community in Battle Harbour, but what there is, is fiercely protected by the people.

It's what scares me about Wyatt leaving for university next year because I know it's not like that everywhere. Or anywhere. The thought of him taking blows from society about who he loves crushes my heart daily.

But I know I have to let him go. I'll support him in whatever way he wants; he knows that.

Being an uncle is tough. But it has some great aspects to it, although Wyatt trying to get me to talk about my dating life is not one of them.

"You should try it sometime," Wyatt wheedles.

"What? Asking Brody to the Halloween party? Nice guy, but not really my type," I tease.

"Ugh! Don't even joke about that. You're way too old for him."

"That is true."

"You're so old you need to go on a date."

"I don't have time to date."

"You don't have time *not* to date. You're getting old."

"Thirty is not old."

"It is when you're sixteen."

The light is fading as we make our way to the viewing spot. The trees on the side of the road are brilliant with their fall colours and leaves skirt across the road as we pass. Wyatt fiddles with the radio, and I feel myself relax after the day.

Fenella

I TAKE A TON of pictures of my new car and post them right away. And then I get behind the wheel.

I bought a car!

It's the best kind of rush.

My phone keeps alerting me to the texts after my car news, but I leave it face down. This is too fun to drive. The Charger purrs and growls, like a wild cat.

I wonder if they have big cats in Laandia, like mountain lions and panthers.

I bet they have bears. What if I see a bear?

Gunnar flew me over Laandia once in his little plane, so I've seen the land from about ten thousand feet, but I've never been outside of the town limits of Battle Harbour. It's very different from a big city that can sprawl for miles—once you get free of the town streets, it's all trees and rocks and the odd house perched on the side of a hill. The town itself might feel small, but outside the settled streets feels wild and wide open, if you can be open while surrounded by towering forests.

I find a very winding road with the ocean crashing against the shore on one side and a lot of big trees on the other.

But I have a car, so I'm happy.

I didn't bother trying to negotiate the price. Coy and Laura need the money more than I do. But I was surprised when Coy pushed the keys at me after I finished my chowder.

I also can't believe they fed me, just like that. I could have been anyone, and they invited me in and gave me soup. Who does that?

"I can't take it now. I don't have the money with me," I told him. "I can bring it tomorrow."

"I figure a model staying at the castle should be good for it. Take it tonight, drop the money off here tomorrow or the next day, whenever you get it sorted," Coy said.

And he just gave me the car to take tonight.

So of course I have to go for a drive.

The headlights sweep along the road, illuminating the rocky shoreline that leads me out of town and up the cliff where the castle sits watching. I pass it and keep going. The farther away from town, the more trees there are. I catch glimpses of the water now and again.

I make a mental note to change the presets on the radio, or subscribe to Sirius, although I've never had to do either of those things before. There's also no Bluetooth for me to sync my phone, so I end up listening to a station that plays twangy country music.

Not my first choice, but driving always needs music. And at least it's not Opium.

I bought a car. I own a car now.

To think, earlier today I was so bored that I debated calling my father to ask if I could come home, and now I'm happy to be in Laandia again. Retail therapy always helps my mood, but the boost buying the car gave me is like a drug. I can get used to this.

What isn't helping my mood is the car in front of me.

This could be a fun road—curving and winding around the cliff. I keep driving up and up, so it'll be amazing coming down. I've driven the California highway, Sea to Sky in British Columbia, and Autobahn, and this road might be up there.

If I can pass this guy.

I caught up to the fossil in the beat-up Corolla taking their own sweet time a few kilometres past the castle and there hasn't been a straight part where I can pass him.

It's a little frustrating.

Finally, they signal and turn on a deserted-looking gravel road. I fly by with a roar, but once I hit the next curve, I think maybe I should figure out where I'm going. The sky has darkened since I left town, a dark purple and I have no idea where I am. Or what is around here. Like bears. Or another castle.

I turn around to head back to find the gravel road and see if they're friendly and can tell me where the heck I am.

My headlights show the white Corolla parked in the middle of a clearing and two men taking something from the trunk. Closer to the water, a lighthouse rears up into the sky, bright light stretching far out into the ocean.

I didn't expect a lighthouse, but I also never expected that one of the men would be Silas from the coffee shop.

He puts up a hand against the bright lights as I park beside him. "Fenella?" he asks with surprise as I bounce out of my new car. "What are you doing here?"

"I bought a car. You like?" Silas stands with a younger version of himself and I smile at the expressions of shock on their faces. "What are you doing out here?"

"That's Coy Schmidt's car," the younger version says.

"It is. He's an interesting one, don't you think? I bought it about an hour ago." I don't feel like getting into the fact I technically haven't bought it *yet* because that's just semantics. It's still my car.

It's surprising how possessive I feel about it.

"You just went out and bought a car? He's been trying to sell the thing for years," Silas says in a warning voice. He pulls a case out of the trunk and shuts it.

"And I have no idea why no one scooped it up. A little pricey, but when you think about all the work he must have put into it, it's worth it. It's a 2007 and it looks fabulous." I give a little shimmy as I pat the hood.

Silas leans against the Corolla, which looks like such a *baby* car next to my yellow beast. I mean, it's a fine car, but it's no Charger. "You sound like you know about cars."

What I don't know about is how *cold* it is here. When the sun disappeared, it took every last bit of warmth with it, and that wind blowing from the ocean would freeze the balls off a buffalo, as Gunnar used to say. I can see why he'd say that now. It's only October but *brr*.

I've never been to Laandia in the winter—and I don't want to. "My father makes toy cars. I can find my way around an engine," I tell Silas proudly, beginning to button my jacket with chilled fingers.

"Those are model cars. I don't think they have actual engines," he points out. But he's smiling as he says it—at least I think it's a smile.

It's nice; people are usually too intimidated or afraid of me to let their guard down so quickly. I smile in return and tell myself it's only to make Silas more comfortable. "Yes, but my father commissions Ford and Dodge to make life-sized models of the best-selling toy cars." Silas raises his eyebrows like that is news to him. Doesn't everyone know that? "There are some collectors who want to drive the real thing."

"I'm sure they do."

People always underestimate my knowledge about cars. I get it—this outfit is not what a grease monkey would wear. "Now, your turn," I say to get back to the question at hand. "Do you often steal away and go parking in the middle of nowhere with...?" I glance at his... son? Both have curly hair and wide eyes and the same smile. They could be father and son.

Silas has a son?

Silas might have a gaggle of sons with three different wives for all I know.

"This is Wyatt. My nephew."

Nephew is better than son, and the news steals the prickle of unease. "Hello, Nephew Wyatt." I smile at him. "So, what are you boys doing up here? Wherever here is? That's why I stopped. I might be a little lost."

"Has Gunnar never taken you up the coast?" Silas asks.

"Gunnar has taken me to the bars in Battle Harbour. That's about it."

Silas shakes his head. "There's a lot more to Laandia than what you can find in Battle Harbour." He points to the lighthouse in the distance. "That's the Double Island Lighthouse. I'm trying to get it recognized as a Dark Sky Location so we can create the first Starlight Reserve in Laandia."

"Dark Sky what?"

"It's a light-pollution-free zone. If you notice, all the outdoor lights face the ground and the bulbs are yellow. Also, this light doesn't flash. It's better for the nocturnal animals in the area, but also—" He points up. "Stars."

Stars. So many stars, and it's still only dusk. There are so many that it's like they're hanging from the ceiling in a cheesy teen rom-com prom movie.

I stand, head tilted back, and take them in. Looking up at them kind of takes my breath away.

"Pretty," Wyatt says. He even sounds like Silas, except his voice isn't as deep yet.

"There are places up the coast that you can see the aurora borealis," Silas continues.

I bring my attention back to him. "I've seen them in Iceland. Beautiful."

"Of course you have." But there's no condescending note in his tone. "I think it would bring in more tourism to the country if we had someplace like the observatory in Nova Scotia.

"Does the country need more tourists?"

"More tourists mean more business and that's always a good thing."

For the first time, I look at Silas as a business owner, rather than the good-looking guy who makes me coffee. "I guess so."

"You can see Neptune tonight," Wyatt cuts in. "Want to check it out?"

"I'm sure Fenella has better things to do," Silas tells him.

"Actually, I don't." I have a new car and nowhere to go with it. It's a little pathetic. "I'm ready to check out anything."

Silas studies me. And I study him right back, the lights from the lighthouse giving the scene a yellowish glow.

I didn't think he was so tall. Not as big as the princes, but they really grow them big here in Laandia.

Silas fits into Coffee for the Sole perfectly—the flannel shirts rolled up to show strong forearms, the smile that's not quite perfect but still causes a flutter, and the ease at which he tops a latte with his special unicorn foam. He's the perfect hero for a small-town coffee shop.

But out here in the dark, wearing a thick corduroy jacket and a beanie tamping down his wavy hair, he's like a different man.

More of a *man*. A manly man. A nothing-like-Tiger-man.

Silas would tower over Tiger, with shoulders double the size.

Now, why am I comparing Silas to Tiger? Even without really knowing, I can tell Silas is the better man.

Is he going to tell me to go home?

I don't want to go home. Or back to the castle. I want to stay here. With Silas.

But before he says anything, Silas unlocks his trunk again. "If you're going to hang around, you need something warmer to wear."

"This is all I've got," I tell him, trying not to let my teeth chatter.

He pulls out something bulky. "You can wear this." He holds it up and I see that it's a thick and heavy-looking parka with a fur-lined hood. Canada Goose jacket? Moose Knuckles? Whatever brand, I'm going to swim in it.

But as he holds it up, I turn around to let Silas help me into it, slipping it on over mine. The coat itself is chilly from being in his trunk, but it cuts the cold, and immediately, I feel less like I'm about to get frostbite. "Thank you."

I fumble to find the zipper and Silas hunches his shoulders to do it up for me. "It's a bit big," he says ruefully.

"And definitely not *your* usual attire," Wyatt chimes in with a laugh.

"But it will keep you warm." And then Silas pulls a wool beanie out of the pocket of the coat and tugs it over my head, *without giving a thought to my hair.*

My hair, which is trapped inside this bulky bear of a coat. Silas realizes it at the same time and slides his hands around my neck to free my long hair, unfolding it so it hangs over my shoulders.

I stand still and stare up at him because only stylists have ever put a coat on me, and no one has ever thought to free my hair. He smooths the hat with big hands. "Sorry," he says with a start. "I didn't mean—"

"It's fine," I say, suddenly breathless. "I'm warm now."

"Good. Let's go see some stars."

Silas

THIS MEANS NOTHING.

Fenella is bored and curious and this means nothing.

Except, as many times as I repeat myself, I can't bring myself to ignore the flare of hope as she follows us up the path into the woods.

She looks adorable wearing my coat. And the hat...

Dead leaves cover the trail and make it impossible to move quietly. I set up solar lights every few metres, but Fenella still follows close behind, reaching out with a hand against my back when we hit a dark patch.

"Should I be nervous?" she asks with an odd tone in her voice that may be actual nerves. "I have no idea where we're going, even if I could see in the dark."

"Afraid I'm about to kidnap you?"

"Serial killer did cross my mind."

"Trust me. I thought you said I was a nice guy."

"Nice guys can still lose people in the dark."

I huff a laugh and Wyatt twists his neck to shoot a surprised look at me. *What*? I mouth, but there's no way for him to see me in the dark.

We step out of the trees a moment later.

I found this spot years ago, a clearing in the woods where the rocks hang over the shoreline, the waves crashing a few feet below. One huge rock is forming a table where I can set up my telescope.

"Wow," Fenella breathes. My eyes have adjusted to the dimness so I can take in her wide eyes. "It's like I'm at the edge of the world."

"Technically, you're at the edge of Laandia," Wyatt says. "This might be the most eastern point of the country. Careful, don't go too close to the edge." We both reach for her as she takes a step.

"I keep meaning to build some sort of barrier there," I add, letting my hand slide off the coat sleeve.

"The ocean is *right* there," she says with delight. "I could jump in."

"There's rocks. So, maybe not."

Fenella pulls out her phone and takes a bunch of pictures, posing with Wyatt as they chatter away while I set up my Celestron Omni double refractor. It's the third telescope I've owned and my favourite.

"I can tag you in these," she says to him. "Your followers will skyrocket if I'm in your feed."

"He's sixteen," I point out. "He doesn't need any more followers or even reasons to be on social media."

"Fair. I'll just post the sky because it is a-*ma*-zing. Unless you want in on this?" She points her phone at me, but I shake my head.

I'm not sure what to say to Fenella. Me, who can talk to anyone and pride myself on making anyone feel comfortable, have suddenly become tongue-tied when I'm around Fenella Carrington.

She's just a woman. I know lots of women and I can talk to them all. Princess Lyra is a personal friend. My cousin Edie is going to be queen of Laandia someday. I once served coffee to Taylor Swift's best friend.

But none of them are Fenella.

"This is just *here* for anyone to see." She tilts her head up, turning in a circle and seemingly enraptured by the vista above.

She should be—it's one of the best spots in the world to look at the stars.

"Do you bring all your girls here?" Fenella ends up beside me, standing very close.

I drop the bag with the extra lens. I'd rather she be close to me than fall over the edge, but she's very distracting.

And I have a feeling she likes to be that way.

"Ah, I... No. Not really."

"I don't know why not. It's the perfect spot." She stares out into the night, the waves a soothing backdrop. My heart gives a traitorous stutter at how peaceful she looks. Every time I see Fenella, she is moving. Constantly active, constant changing expressions. But now she's still, and her smile...

Stop looking at her smile. She gives the same smile to everyone.

Imagine living each day like it's an adventure. Imagine having the money to do so.

"Can you see whales from here?" she asks, peering over to look into the dark water.

I forget about the telescope and grab her wrist, letting my fingers slide down to cup her hand and leading her a safe step closer to the edge. The rock does drop off unexpectedly but I've been here enough times to know the feel of it.

"Whales, icebergs," Wyatt tells her. "Grandpa is convinced he once saw all the way to Scotland on a clear day."

"He didn't see Scotland," I chide.

"He might have. It's the closest to us, just over there." He stretches out his arm and points over the gray sea.

"Do you know all the stars?" Fenella points up, her hand still in mine. I'm not sure if she realizes it, but I'm very aware—of how small and soft her hand. How cold her fingers are.

Her fingers move, but instead of pulling her hand away, she entwines her fingers with mine.

I'm standing at the edge of the world, holding hands with Fenella Carrington.

"Not all of them," Wyatt concedes. "But a lot. That's Cassiopeia." He stretches his arm up and out. "Perseus. And that's

Lynx there. You can see the Lyra constellation, but you have to stay here for a while and it gets pretty cold."

"Lyra has a star named after her? I've never heard of that." She turns to me. "Is this what you do here? Teach him how to name the stars?"

"Silas was supposed to be an astronaut," Wyatt says before I can answer. "He gave up the idea when I came along, because my mom is an idiot and took off and left me with my grandparents. Which is stupid, because I'm not his kid. He's an awesome uncle, though."

"I bet he is." Fenella smiles but I see the curiosity in her eyes. "He can still go up into space," she adds. "Jeff Bezos, Elon Musk—lots of spaceships go up and check things out."

"Like I can afford that." Fenella and Wyatt look at each other. "No," I say. "Please don't think you can buy me a seat on a spaceship."

"I probably could," she whispers. "But, whatever."

"It's not being in space, it's just... seeing... this." I spread an arm out. "Stars."

"It's his thing," Wyatt adds.

"It's a good thing," Fenella agrees. "I thought coffee was just your thing, so this is a plus. Show me something."

I reluctantly let go of her hand to check the sights in the telescope and make adjustments until Neptune is visible, hanging low and clear in the scope. "Take a look," I offer.

Fenella eagerly bends to peer into the eyepiece. "Oh, my god," she cries, her voice echoing over the water and loud enough to startle something in the trees. "That's a planet."

"I told you that you can see Neptune tonight," Wyatt says smugly, like he pulled it from the sky to present it to her.

She straightens to look at me. "Can you see it all the time?"

"No, it depends on the rotation of the Earth and the other planets. Usually, Venus is visible." I move the telescope and Fenella eagerly bends to look. "That's Venus."

"That's Venus," she echoes. "I'm looking at a planet. I'm looking at a *planet*. It's beautiful."

Wyatt nudges my arm and gives me a knowing expression. I shake my head. *Hot*, he mouths.

I almost laugh because whatever Fenella looks like wearing my ten-year-old coat that is warm and so unfashionable—and probably smells a bit funky from living in my trunk—is not *hot*.

Definitely cute, but not hot.

I thought you liked boys, I mouth back.

He points to me and then Fenella, like I have no idea what he's getting at. I know exactly what he's getting at, and I want no part of it.

That's what I keep telling myself.

Fenella straightens up. "What else is up here? Here, you can look," she offers to Wyatt.

"I see Venus all the time. Neptune is pretty cool." I'm proud of the way he moves the telescope into the right position and makes the necessary adjustments before taking a look.

"You spend a lot of time together?" Fenella asks.

I glance over, see the way she's looking at me with those purple eyes, and nod.

"Your mom not around?" Fenella asks as casually as if she's asking about the weather.

"No." Even after all this time, Wyatt's tone is still bitter but much better than when he was younger and someone mentioned his mother. The tween years were particularly difficult for him. "Definitely not around."

"That can't feel good."

"No, it really doesn't."

"You know what else doesn't feel good?" Fenella asks as she leans down to take another look. "When your mom is around but clearly doesn't want to be. When she makes everything and everyone feel more important than you. But you wouldn't know about that because you've got this really cool uncle and a great set of grandparents who consider you the most important thing in their world."

There's a long pause. "Yeah," Wyatt says finally. "I do."

"You do," she agrees. "The mother thing has to suck, though. But focus on the good things that are going on with your life instead of dwelling on the bad stuff."

"Is that what you do?"

"Oh, I wasn't talking about myself." And then she winks at Wyatt, who breaks into a fangirl—fanguy—smile.

"You're a lot cooler than I thought you'd be," he concedes.

"Oh, I am the coolest," she corrects. "Want to do a selfie?" And she poses with him, both with big grins. "Tag me if you want to increase your followers. Oops, no don't, or Uncle Silas will be upset with me. How did you find this spot?" she asks me.

"I've lived in Battle Harbour my entire life. There's not a lot of spots that I don't know about."

"What's your favourite spot?" she demands. "The best place to look at stars or bring girls or—"

Wyatt snorts. "He doesn't bring girls anywhere."

"Like I would tell you."

"It's a small town," Wyatt says in a dry voice. "I'd know if you were dating."

"I date." I glance down at Fenella, who watches me with an expectant expression. "I date."

A corner of her mouth lifts like she's trying not to smile. "Where would be your favourite place to take a date then?"

Right here, but I don't say that out loud. I've only brought one woman here and it didn't mean much to her. That kind of spoiled it for anyone else, but now that Fenella seems to be enjoying herself...

"There are a couple of good restaurants in town," I tell her.

"Really? You know *all the spots* and you'd take a girl to a restaurant?"

"Where's that place you used to take Mia?" Wyatt is still looking into the telescope, so he doesn't see my jolt from Mia's name.

I hope Fenella doesn't notice.

Four years, and I still react when I hear her name. I know that's because I haven't let myself move on, or get over her, or picture a future that doesn't have her in it.

I feel the weight of Fenella's gaze on me. I shrug.

"What about you?" she asks Wyatt. "Who are you dating?"

"I asked Brody to the Halloween dance."

"I don't know who that is, but sounds great."

"Is that all that interests you?" Wyatt asks. "Who is dating is who?"

"Around here? I have to be interested in something."

"Why are you here, then?"

"Because the guy *I* was dating turned out to be an idiot. Let me have another turn."

They take turns looking and pointing and I tell them what's out there.

When she's not looking through the lens, Fenella moves back to my side.

I lose track of how long we stay there because Fenella keeps asking questions like she's truly interested. But eventually, I realize that she's hovering by me, attaching herself to my side really, when she's not looking through the scope, because she's shivering.

"We should go," I finally say reluctantly. When I'm one with the stars—corny, sure, but that's how I feel—I never want it to end, but it's different with Fenella here.

I'm having fun with her. I'm enjoying her company.

Not that Fenella doesn't have things that would be enjoyable—her company, that's all I'm thinking about—but I never thought it would be *me* who enjoyed it. Her. Spending time with her.

She's Fenella Carrington, after all.

So I drink in all of her smiles, and excited exclamations. She seems fascinated by the proximity of the ocean, demanding to know what animals we've seen and where we saw them.

I think she really wants to jump off the table rock and I explain a few times what she could expect if she did—icy cold water, strong undertow, rocks hidden under the surface, and probable death. Wyatt tells her about the spot near town where the kids swim, jumping off the rocks into a sandy-bottomed bay, and she promises to come back in the summer so he can take her.

I'm not going to hold my breath for that to happen. I may be enjoying her company, but I'm not going to kid myself that there will be a repeat of it.

I do like how she seems excited about so many things. Maybe it's an act, or maybe Fenella actually lives a sheltered life—as a billionaire.

Giving everyone one last look at Neptune, I pack up the telescope, setting it gently in the case. Wyatt leads us back through the trees, the dim solar-powered lights illuminating parts of the path.

"Do you come here often?" Fenella asks, her voice low because we're walking through the woods at night and it always feels like you should be quiet. Despite this, her question comes across as somewhat seductive. Flirtatious.

She realizes it at the same time and gives a laugh. "That came out wrong."

"No, it's good... I do come here often. As much as I can."

"You really must like stars."

"I do. Almost as much as I like coffee," I tease.

"I didn't... I don't have anything like that," she confesses. "Nothing that would bring me out to the woods in the middle of the night."

"It's only ten-thirty," Wyatt informs us.

"Still." Fenella lifts her hands and the sleeves of my jacket shift and slip down her arms. "Nothing."

"You must have interests."

"Yes, but I don't have a passion."

"What do you do when you're not hiding out in the castle?"

"You've seen my Instagram. That's what I do." She sounds... disappointed almost. "A little bit of everything and not much of anything." She pauses for a long moment and just when I think she's finished, she starts again, her words rushed together. "I wanted to work at my father's company. I think I'd be good at it, really make a difference, but with everything that happened—the video with Tiger going viral and the last video, and the last—my father said the board doesn't want me. Not now, anyway. They think I have too high a profile and I need to stay out of sight."

"Laandia to the rescue, then, huh?" I keep it light so I don't let on how hearing that makes me feel—how the sadness and disappointment in Fenella's voice cuts straight to my heart.

I never imagined I would ever feel sympathy for her.

We step out of the woods, into the clearing where the cars are parked. The moon hangs high in the sky and the strong light from the lighthouse lets me see Fenella—and I realize how adorable she looks wearing my coat. Box-like, but lumpy, and the moonlight seems to send sparkles cascading through her long, black hair. "You couldn't have found a better place to hide out," I add.

"Gunnar didn't even hesitate," Fenella says. "Jumped in his plane and came and got me. And King Magnus made sure no press will be let in, so whatever I do here, I get to do in private."

"And what are you thinking of doing here?" Now my voice sounds slightly seductive. Flirtatious. "I mean..."

Fenella laughs.

"Or who?" Wyatt cackles, sounding more like a sixty-year-old woman than a sixteen-year-old man-boy.

"Recent bad break-up, remember? I hadn't given that much thought," Fenella says with a twist of her lips. "But now that I have my car, I have options. And... maybe people, now, for those options."

People? Like... me, people?

Fenella glances up at the sky, but I look at her. At the length of her neck. At those cheekbones that sell things, like handbags.

I think other things sold the handbags, but since the rest of her is completely covered, I'll say it's the cheekbones.

"Look! A shooting star," Fenella cries.

"A satellite," I tell her without taking my eyes off her.

She does a little jump. "No—look." She grabs my arm and hoists it up to force me to look where she's pointing. I pull my gaze away from her pink cheeks, and yes, slightly blue-tinged lips, just in time to see the tail end of a falling star. "I've never seen one before."

Her first falling star. Normally, that would be a gift for me, but all I can think about is that Fenella is cold.

And what I could do to warm her up.

"Make a wish," Wyatt calls.

I know what I'm wishing for.

Fenella glances over at me, catching me in her violet gaze, and I wonder again how a person can have purple eyes.

But then I stop wondering because Fenella doesn't drop her gaze. She looks like she wants—

She looks at my mouth and it's as if she skims a finger along my lips.

I tell myself it's my imagination.

Only it's not.

Fenella

THE NEXT MORNING, THE sun wakes me in my suite of rooms in the castle because I forgot to pull the curtains again. They're heavy and long and a pain to close, so I'm up earlier than expected this morning.

Gunnar told me Camille stayed in the same room before they married, so I'm a little puffed that this is a room fit for a princess. But would Camille still be considered a princess if Odin abdicated his position in the line of succession?

These are things I don't need to think about. Or do I have the bandwidth to consider because I wake up thinking of Silas?

He gave me his coat.

The thick lump lies on the end of my bed—it's no Moose Knuckles, not even a Canada Goose. Some no-name brand that I would never deign to look at in the regular world, let alone wear.

But Silas gave it to me to wear because I was cold.

Maybe I wake up thinking about him because of the scent emanating from it. It definitely smells like coffee. I lie there for a few minutes until I push off the covers.

The floor is freezing under my bare feet. I need to remember to wear socks to bed, but I was warm last night when I returned to the castle. Overheated, maybe, since I wore the coat in the car, with the heat turned up full.

I pull on the coat in front of the mirror. It's a non-descript grey-brown, hanging almost to my knees. It's huge. Is this what I looked like last night? I zip the coat up and it's all coat—all winter coat and no me. I flip up the hood; my hands have vanished and only my pink satin pyjama pants stick out the bottom.

It smells of coffee and Silas, pine—or cedar maybe. A tree smell. But there's something else, something salty. The sea?

Salted caramel? Does Silas smell that sweet? And why should my stomach give a little lurch that I know what he smells like now?

Did I actually appear in public like this?

No, I wore a beanie. A toque, they call them here, which makes it worse. I have to push back the hood to find the brown knitted hat. It's rough in my hands but once on my head—

I don't look that bad. I'm Fenella Carrington. I can make anything look good. Some of the outfits I've worn modelling were worse than this, and far less warm.

I free my hair from the heavy fabric like Silas did.

No man has ever given me their coat when I was cold. That may be because I live in a warmer climate, but still. Gunnar offered me his suit jacket once when we were out for dinner in London, but that was in the early stages of our relationship and photographers had followed us. We both knew what the optics of me wearing his jacket would be.

But Silas never hesitated or had an ulterior motive. He's a nice guy who knew I was cold, and I never expected him to give me his coat—or insist on I wear it back to the castle.

I didn't expect any of what happened last night. I bought a car and saw some beautiful stars at the edge of Laandia and Silas gave me his coat to wear because it was frigid cold.

I wondered what it would be like to kiss him.

When Wyatt told me to make a wish because I saw a *shooting star*, my mind went right to that mouth, and what it would be like to kiss Silas.

I have kissed a lot of men in my life. Some have meant something. Most haven't.

I have also seen a lot of beautiful things in this world, so a simple shooting star shouldn't have had me jumping like I got a present. Billionaires don't react to beauty—we act like it was put there for our benefit. That view from Lake Como? Of course it's for me. Seeing the northern lights in Iceland? I paid to be there, so it was expected.

But the unexpectedness of the night did something to me. Made me think of Silas in a way that I never really considered him.

He did that for me.

Not that it was planned; it was a random coincidence that I was even there at the same time as he was but still.

Silas is...

Not for me.

Seriously, there's no way I would be good for him. My life would eat him up and spit him out. There's no way sweet Silas could handle the real me out in the real world.

Sometimes I can barely handle myself.

But I still wake up thinking of that almost-moment when we could have—

Yeah. We could have. And it would have been nice.

Maybe better than the shooting star.

I hug Silas's coat and, for the first time in a long time, have that little jump of excitement when I think about seeing someone.

When I get to the dining room where the cook has set out breakfast, that little jump of excitement hops away because Edie is at the table.

I met Edie when I came for Prince Odin's wedding back in June. At that time, Edie was a "friend" of Prince Kalle's. I stress the friend because I had a few moments with Kalle while I was here.

There were a few dances at the wedding, possibly a kiss or two, and then a dinner. That was it. Kalle is Gunnar's older brother, and while I have no qualms about most families, I was not putting myself in the middle of a healthy, brotherly relationship. Plus, things with Tiger were off-and-on back then.

I never should have flipped the switch back to on with Tiger. Things shouldn't have continued with Kalle, but I should have shut it right down with Tiger.

I tell myself it won't be awkward with Edie when I find her seated at the table.

"Hey, there," I say.

Since when do I say "hey, there"? Awkward.

"Fenella." Edie smiles, her dark eyes warm and fully awake at this hour. "Good morning."

I pour myself a coffee and survey what's available. Food has been laid out on a sideboard by the door, and the scent of it has my stomach rumbling. Silver serving dishes of eggs and bacon, fresh bagels, and a display of fruit take the centre of the table, with carafes of coffee and hot tea.

I've stayed in more luxurious places and eaten better food, but there is something about the castle that makes me feel at home. When Gunnar invited me to stay, I didn't have to think twice before I agreed. I may not feel like I belong in the small town of Battle Harbour, but King Magnus and his family have always made me feel welcome whenever I have visited.

I ready a plate for myself and sit down across from Edie.

She and Kalle are now more than friends, i.e. engaged to be married—and a real engagement unlike the half-assed one I had with Tiger—and I can't notice much of a change. Edie is still uber-casual, wearing jeans and a sweatshirt that's seen better days. I'd be alarmed at her wardrobe, since by all accounts, she's going to be the next queen of Laandia, but King Magnus dresses worse than she does.

Would I have wanted to be queen of Laandia if things worked out with Kalle? It might have been fun... for a while. But I can't see it happening.

"Is Kalle joining you?" I ask Edie, then kick myself. Is she going to think I'm looking forward to seeing him?

This is why I don't keep in touch with my exes. Gunnar and I figured out how to stay friends, but Kalle and I weren't enough to even call him an ex.

I'm really making it awkward, and I rarely make anything awkward.

Edie shakes her head. "He has an early meeting, which is why we were here last night. It's easier to stay in town when I have to close the pub."

"I'm glad the two of you got together."

"I'm glad it didn't work out with the two of you." Her smile takes any sting out of the words.

"It wouldn't have. I'm not queen material."

Edie raises her cup. "Sometimes I wonder if I am," she says ruefully.

I study Edie across the table. The polite thing would be to reassure her that yes, she'll make a great queen. And she probably will. But if I know anything, it's how important public perception is. And if Edie keeps looking like a contestant from a bag lady competition, no one will think much of her other qualities.

"If you ever need some advice—" I tread carefully. "About dealing with the public or fashion or style, let me know."

"Yeah." Edie winces. "Mrs. Theissen has been trying to work on my image before the wedding. The only problem is I don't like the image she's trying to make. I see Magnus and—"

"Men can look however they want," I point out. "Women are criticized for everything."

"True." She looks down at her sweatshirt. "I need something in between stuffy and just rolled out of bed."

"We could go shopping while I'm here," I offer. "If it's not too weird for you."

Making plans to go shopping with the future queen of Laandia while dining at a castle. This is my life.

"It wouldn't be too weird for *me*," Edie says with the confidence of winning the heir to the Laandian throne. "But, sure. That would be... maybe not *fun* because I'm not much for shopping... but helpful."

"Let me know when. My schedule is open."

"How long are you staying?"

I sigh. Yesterday's text to my father asking that same question came back with *at least another week, still showing up in the feeds*. But that didn't upset me as much as I thought it would. "I'm not sure," I admit. "Hiding out might take longer than expected."

"That's what you're doing? Hiding out?"

"The board of my father's company sees my actions as an embarrassment," I tell Edie in a cool voice. "And since I'm trying to get on their good side, the less they see of me, the better."

"But you didn't do anything wrong. From what I heard, that Cougar guy cheated on you."

"Tiger," I correct with a smile. "But no one seems to realize that. They see my temper tantrum and that's it."

Edie snorts. "That was no temper tantrum. If Kalle pulled anything like that, I wouldn't throw something at him, I'd throw him out a window of his precious pub."

I've seen firsthand how Edie deals with obnoxious drunks and despite the fact all of the Laandian princes are built like trees, she could do it. "The daughter of the president and CEO of Carrington Toys needs to keep up appearances. Apparently," I say wryly.

"That's bull—a lot of bull stuff. But I guess I need to get used to that. Appearances and all that."

"I think you'll have an easier time. Laandia is a lot more forgiving than the board of Carrington."

Edie grins. "But I could still use some help. So, thanks. Shopping? Tomorrow morning?"

I lift my cup. "I will make the time." It's nice to have a plan. But it's more than that—I've missed having my friends around. Edie and I aren't friends—yet—but it's a start.

"What else have you been doing?" she asks as she sips her coffee.

"Not much of anything," I confess. "I bought a car."

"You *bought* a car."

"It seemed easier than renting one. It's a Dodge Charger. It's yellow."

"You bought Coy Schmidt's car?"

"Yes, him. Strange name."

"Strange man. Are you sure the car is a good one?"

"My brother isn't the only one who knows about cars. I took it for a drive last night and it runs great. I ended up at this lighthouse." I hesitate for a moment. "Silas was there."

"Looking at the stars." She smiles as she stands to refill our cups. "He's our one-man NASA. He should have been an astronaut but it's not like we have a space program."

"He seems to know a lot about what's up there. He was telling me names—"

Edie's eyes snap to attention. "He took you star-gazing?"

"There was no real taking. I was there, he was there. Nephew Wyatt was there too. Why?"

Suddenly shrewd brown eyes study me. "Silas is a great guy. One of the best." Edie's tone turns cool and cautious.

One of the best. And I'm not. That's what Edie is getting at.

"He seems nice," I offer.

"*Very* nice. We're cousins, so I'm biased. There's no one to compare to him around here."

"So where's the Mrs. Silas?"

Edie sighs as she adds milk and sugar. "There was someone a few years ago," she admits. "Mia Khan. They were completely and utterly in love, but then she wanted to leave Battle Harbour for some reason. And Silas wouldn't hear about it, and so she left without him."

"Why wouldn't he leave if they were so perfect?"

"Wyatt. And the coffee shop. Silas is extremely loyal. Family is all for him."

More than the love of his life? Hmm... I'd do a lot for Ashton, but not give up on love. And one of Silas's expressions from last night makes me wonder if that's what he's done.

Because look at the man—he's the whole package.

"Wyatt seems like a cool kid," I offer.

"He's more like his son. Have you heard about Silas's sister?"

I'm finished with my bagel but stay put if Edie is about to spill the tea. "Not a lot, but Wyatt made it sound like she took off."

"He was four months old. Emily was seventeen and wanted nothing to do with having a baby. She... I think it's probably better that she left," she finishes. "Silas and his parents gave Wyatt more stability than Emily ever could."

"She's never been back?"

"Never once in sixteen years. And no one was really surprised. Silas was fourteen when she left, and he was just devastated. He adored her. His parents too. She broke their hearts, and never coming home is just cruel."

"Sounds like it." I couldn't imagine abandoning Ashton like that, let alone a baby.

"When Mia left, it was like it happened all over again," Edie continues. "Silas was a mess for a long time. He still hasn't started dating again."

"That's... a long time."

"It is, and he's such a great guy." She looks at me warily. "You're not interested in him, are you?"

"I..."

"Not that you're not a good person, but you'll eventually leave. I don't want him to have to deal with that again."

Edie's concerns are loud and clear, and I get it. She's worried Silas will be hurt.

By me.

While I might not leave a trail of broken hearts in my wake, there have been a few. I have a habit of ducking out of relationships first because if I don't, Tiger happens. As in, I get hurt.

I don't like being hurt. I don't react well, and it makes me look bad.

I also don't like being told what to do, and that seems to be what Edie is doing. "I'm only here for another week or so," I tell her, ignoring the sudden, jangling pang at the thought of going home.

Why wouldn't I want to go home? That's the whole point of me being here—to go home.

"It's not like he'll fall for me in that time," I add, which makes me laugh. Men have fallen for me in much less time than that.

The cousin of the Italian prince spent six hours with me before he proposed. It's very possible that Silas has already fallen for me.

I don't hate that thought. In fact, it makes a cozy ball of warmth in my chest. Silas. And me.

But if what Edie says is true, that puts me in the prime position to hurt him.

And I really don't like that thought.

SILAS

I WOULD RATHER NOT see Fenella today.

Last night was... strange. Strangely good.

There was a moment there at the end when I wondered what it would be like to kiss her. To feel those full lips under mine, those purple eyes closing...

I haven't kissed a girl in a long time. Too long.

Embarrassingly long.

If I'm going to start kissing anyone, it shouldn't be Fenella.

Because Fenella is a party girl who blew into town and she'll blow right out in a few days. In the meantime, I'll serve her coffee and not talk about what is in the sky at night. Or even find out if her mouth is as soft as it looks.

She will drop out of sight soon enough and I'll never see her again.

Like Mia. And my sister.

Not seeing her is a good plan.

Only, mid-morning when I come back from the stock room with a sleeve of cups in my hand, Fenella is at the counter talking with Leodie.

My hand gives an instinctive squeeze, like I have her hand in mine. Only I squeeze harder until I realize I've crushed the cups with my grip.

"Hi, Star Guy," Fenella calls. Her smile is warm and directed straight at me.

I kind of feel like that falling star from last night. The one I wished on—wished I'd get a chance to find out how soft Fenella's lips are.

This morning they're covered by some sort of shiny gloss. It's plum coloured.

This is bad. I should not care about what her lips look like.

"How's your drama-filled day?" Fenella asks as I contemplate what I should not be caring about.

She's holding my coat in her arms and the sight of that—and only that—is why I give her such a big smile. Because she's here to bring it back to me, and that's it. "Good," I say, looking everywhere except her face. At those lips I could have kissed last night.

"Bad," Leodie corrects as she makes Fenella's latte. "He's doing double shifts until we can find someone. And I suspect he was out late last night." She frowns at me like a nursemaid.

"I brought your coat back." But she continues to hold it.

Leodie's frown flips upside down. "Why does Fenella have your coat, Silas?"

"He showed me the stars," Fenella says, looking straight at me. "And it was cold."

"He showed you..." Leodie's face all but dances with glee.

"It wasn't planned," I cut in.

"I was lost," Fenella adds.

"You weren't lost. That road would have taken you... okay, maybe you would have gotten a little lost." I grin ruefully at her, doing my best to ignore the expression on Leodie's face.

She's watching our exchange like she watches the latest episode of Emily in Paris. I know this, because I caught her watching on her break once.

"You saved me," Fenella says. "Plus, we saw a falling star."

Like I need the reminder.

"That sounds *romantic*," Leodie says with a little too much happiness. "Now I get why you look so wiped this morning. It's not the double shifts at all." Leodie gives me a knowing glance and I wish another customer would come in to distract her. "Sounds like you had a fun night."

"It was." Fenella is still looking at me, smiling at me with those big purple eyes. It sounds disturbing, but I'm fixated on the colour. "I'm glad you didn't let Nathalia come back," she says, finally turning to Leodie. "She really had no business working here. Trying to put lavender into a pumpkin spice." Fenella shivers. "What's next? Raspberry?"

"That would be a crime," I manage.

"She wouldn't let me teach her anything. She has that Breville espresso maker at home and thought she knew everything." Leodie rolls her eyes as she hands Fenella her pumpkin spice latte. With vanilla. And unicorn froth.

There is no one in line behind her, so Fenella seems happy to stay where she is.

I have more than enough to do, so why am I still standing here with them? I could take my coat and go.

Is it silly how I like the way Fenella cradles it in her arms?

"That's nothing. We have a Victoria Arduino at home and it makes much better foam than the Breville ever could." Fenella sips her latte and hums with pleasure.

I steal a glance at my incredibly expensive espresso maker. "You have one of these?" I set my hand on the gleaming top.

"We don't have the double frother but the same one. I love it. It's the only thing I can use in the kitchen."

"You can use one of these?" Leodie demands. "It was a beast for me to learn. Silas..." she muses with a look in her eye.

"No," I say instinctively. It's the same look she had in her eye when she asked out Reggie Barnes, and that was a disaster.

"No, what?" Fenella asks, those eyes watching over the rim of her cup. "This is really good, by the way."

"No, I am not hiring Fenella to take over from Nathalia. No offence," I add to Fenella.

"There is offence," Fenella cries, her expression morphing from polite smile to excitement. "There is so much offence, because why *wouldn't* you want to hire me?"

Her excitement jars me as much as when I grabbed the handle of the frother when it was running. "You'd want to work here?"

"Yes!" She's actually considering it? "Of course. Why wouldn't I want to work here? You're a nice guy and you'd never fire me, no matter what I messed up."

Leodie laughs along with her.

"Are you forgetting that you have no experience working in a... anywhere? Have you ever had a job?"

Thankfully Fenella isn't offended by my question.

"I'm trying to get a job," she explains. "I've been asking my father to let me take over some of the marketing for the new line."

"Marketing." I nod. That's not a bad thing, but Fenella Carrington working *here?* "Do you have any experience?"

"I market myself. And I'm a very difficult product. But all that's beside the point," she says airily. "I can make a mean coffee. Seriously, no one can make better." Leodie taps the cup on the counter. "Okay, this is pretty good, too. And you make amazing lattes," she concedes. "But I make really good coffee. And my mocha-vanilla-matcha latte is the best."

"That sounds mildly disgusting," Leodie admits. "I'm not a tea person, green or otherwise. But Silas, we need her," she pleads. "At least until you find someone to replace Nathalia. You can't keep working double shifts, especially while Neptune is visible. And the meteor shower coming up as well."

"I saw Neptune," Fenella confides. "It was amazing."

"And he should show it to you again. Silas, you can't work so much. You need to show the stars to our guests from away." I know that gleam in Leodie's eyes but I feel like I'm being dragged along behind one of the boats in the harbour, unable to get out from behind the wake. "We *need* someone else here."

"You do look tired," Fenella offers. But there's a sparkle in her eye like it's a secret between us that she's the reason for the dark circles under my eyes this morning. "I can help out," she adds. "It'll be fun."

I stare at Fenella, waiting for her to finish the sentence. The *but...*

But nothing is coming.

This must be a joke. There's no way Fenella Carrington, daughter of a billionaire, wants to work in my shop. There's no way she wants to work *anywhere*.

But she still stands there, waiting expectantly as Leodie shoots me excited glances.

"What do you know about working in a coffee shop?" I finally manage to ask.

"Not much," Fenella says cheerfully. "Actually, nothing at all. But I already know how to use your machine, plus I really like coffee. And tea. Anything with caffeine. And I like it when you talk stars."

I don't look at Leodie. She's going to have so many questions... "Why would you *want* to work here?" I demand.

"I'm bored." Fenella's reply is simple. "I'm here for at least another week and it would give me something to do. And it will give you time to find someone else. Why would you say no? You don't even have to pay me?"

"Of course, I'll pay you."

"You really don't have to. Just give me all the drinks I want."

"You get that when you work here," Leodie whispers.

"Perfect. It's a win-win. But I need tomorrow morning off to go shopping with Edie."

I laugh because there's nothing else to say. I now realize Fenella Carrington's superpower is her ability to get people to do what she wants.

Only... she wasn't the one who suggested she work for me. In a roundabout way, that was me.

I don't know if I should kick myself, or give myself a pat on the back. "We'll give it a try," I concede.

"Really?" Fenella's expression is one of surprise, but I see the flash of vulnerability like no one had ever given her a chance before. "You made the right choice," she adds, smoothing her surprise into a satisfied smile.

"I said we'll give it a try," I remind her. "You might be another Nathalia."

"Even if I was, you wouldn't fire me." Fenella laughs.

"Don't be so sure." But as she continues to smile at me, and the happiness in her face leaks over to mine, I shrug my shoulders. "Probably not."

Fenella

Me: I got a job!

Lavinia: Why?

Coral: Doing what?

Rupe: Did Daddy C finally agree to hire you?

Me: Not yet, but now I have experience as a barista, how can he say no?

Milo: What has small-town life done to our Fen?

Ashton: Is this to pay for the car?

None of my friends have ever held a job. Nor have they ever wanted to.

I feel like an explorer, setting forth for a new world.

In my yellow Dodge Charger.

Silas invites me behind the counter like he's welcoming me to a party. Or inside a secret club. Or to join a team...

He hired me—sort of.

It doesn't matter. I want this job. I'm excited about something. For the second time in less than twenty-four hours, Silas Bell has snapped me out of what might have ended up being a pity party, had I let it go on, and given me something to look forward to.

And it's a job.

I got a job.

When I was nineteen, I had a fling with a barista who worked at the local Starbucks. My mother was appalled, which is why I did it. Dirk had no idea who my parents were, and I liked it that way. The anonymity I had every time I went to see him was a heady feeling. It made me giddy.

It made me fall for a guy who, even if I had been a regular girl, would have been nothing special.

I feel that way with Silas. Not that he isn't anything special—I'm beginning to think he's the opposite, which is another problem—but the way he treats me like everyone else? Like I'm a regular girl?

It's been a long time since I felt anything close to regular.

Dirk of Starbucks also taught me to love coffee in ways that I have refined in the years since. Being behind the counter at Coffee for the Sole might be like peeking behind the wizard's curtain, but it also feels familiar, like I'm not totally out of place.

The counter that separates those who work the magic and those who drink it is a long slab of dark, fake wood, covered in all sorts of things: cups and lids and sleeves, gift cards and—

"Colouring pages?" I hold up a sheet of paper covered with outlines of fish. "Do you have a lot of customers who come in to colour?"

"No, but we get mothers with little kids who need to be distracted so they can have a moment to enjoy their coffee," Silas tells me. "Why don't we give it a test run? Make me your favourite coffee—not pumpkin spice," he adds quickly.

"Why not pumpkin spice?"

Silas leans in close enough for me to breathe in his Silas scent. "I can't stand the stuff," he admits in a low voice.

"How is that possible? You're autumn personified."

He gives a twist of a smile. "How do you figure?"

"Flannel." I tug at his sleeve. "Constant flannel." Today, he's wearing a red Buffalo plaid shirt and even though I'm not a fan of the fabric, it looks unbelievably cozy with Silas wearing it.

He's my boss. I shouldn't be thinking that anything about him is cozy. Or good smelling.

"That's all it takes to be the personification of a season?" he asks. "Because you look fall trendy today as well."

This morning, I paired my black stove-pipe jeans with a rust-coloured long-sleeved cashmere T-shirt and a wide silver belt. "You have to be careful with this colour," I say, plucking at the material. "Anything more of an orange shade, you end up looking like a pumpkin."

"I doubt you could ever look like a pumpkin, Fenella."

That is admiration in Silas's eyes. I can tell.

"You two about finished here?" Leodie leans against the counter watching us with a questioning smile. "I'm waiting for the test run."

I take a step back. I hadn't realized I had been leaning toward Silas, like a tree preparing to fall.

"Favourite drink." Silas's cheeks are pink. "Not pumpkin spice latte."

"Maybe you just haven't been making it the right way," I muse, elbowing him aside to check out the espresso maker, with the dual handles and steamers. "Shiny."

"Silas's pride and joy."

Beside the machine is a drip coffee maker and a hot water tap for tea. Bottles of syrup and bags of beans line a shorter counter behind me.

There's a distance of about five feet—plenty of room for three people to move around— and yet, I am standing very close to Silas.

Does he even realize he's a distraction? "This isn't my favourite, but it's good." Rifling through the collection of tea bags, I find a ginger and lemon blend as well as turmeric and add both bags to an inch of hot water. Then I steam oat milk until it's frothy and add it to the cup and drizzle a healthy dose of honey and present it on a saucer to Silas.

While he gives a tentative sip, I start making a mochaccino with an extra shot of espresso and chocolate, with cinnamon and chocolate sprinkles. "I don't know how you make the unicorn foam yet," I tell Leodie as I hand her the mug.

"We'll get you set up and then I'll give you a lesson," Leodie promises. She sips at the coffee. "This is good." She hands it to Silas to try and they swap cups.

"So? How did my test run go?" I ask, trying not to sound needy. Because while I've never been a needy person, I really want to work here.

The possibility gives me more of a burst of energy than three lattes.

I've never had an everyday job, like a waitress or a sales clerk, or Maurizio in Monte Carlo, who sells yachts and other boats. I've modelled and... that's about it.

Silas and Leodie have a conversation with just their eyes. "If you really want to, we can see how it goes today," Silas finally says.

"I really want to."

He shakes his head. "I have no idea why," he mutters.

"It'll be fun. *I'm* fun," I promise with a big smile.

Silas opens his mouth like he's about to reply, but closes it without saying anything.

I have a job.

I haven't given much thought to the fact that I have zero work experience. But following Leodie around the shop for the first hour, I discover there is a lot I don't know about dealing with customers.

Like the fact that you have to smile and bite your tongue when they order one cup of tea and two cups of warm water. Or a cup of water for their dog. And when you mess up an order and give them regular milk instead of oat in their frappuccino, you should expect them to come rushing back in to use the restroom fifteen minutes later.

"Hello and welcome to Coffee for the Sole," I chirp at the older woman at the counter who looks like she applied her makeup with a shovel.

Still, she's my real first customer. Leodie gave me the go-ahead to serve her myself. "I'm Fenella, and what can I get you? A pumpkin spice latte? A caramel macchiato? Or how about a flat white with..."

The woman flicks her gaze to Silas with a frightened glance. "Morning, Mrs. Pebbles," he says quickly. "She'll have a flat white, Fenella. And a cinnamon bun?"

"Always," Mrs. Pebbles says.

"I can do a flat white," I tell him.

"I know you can." And Silas smiles down at me.

That distracts me, but I manage, even decorating the micro-foam with a leaf decoration.

Silas has a great smile. I don't love the scruff of beard or the bit of mustache that hasn't quite filled in yet, but the smile is first-rate. It makes his green eyes crinkle. I like that he's so open with it, bestowing it on anyone who comes in the shop, not just a select few.

I like the way he smiles at me.

"Do you know everyone's order?" I demand after Mrs. Pebbles takes her order to a table where she gives half her bun to her overweight dog. People seem to feed pastries to their dogs a lot here.

"If they're regulars."

"How long have you worked here?"

Leodie gives a cough behind me. "He owns it."

I glance around the shop, seeing the tables full of satisfied customers, comfortable to sit and have their coffee. I see the pictures on the wall of long-ago Battle Harbour, the fishing paraphernalia, the cups and plates... and the hominess of the place.

It makes sense that Silas owns it.

"It's not much," he mutters.

"It's everything," Leodie argues. "This place is the cornerstone of the town. Silas took over ten years ago when his parents retired and doubled the income within a year. It was great with Mr. and Mrs. Bell but—"

"You made it your own," I interrupt. "You made it... home. It feels like home. Friendly and comfortable and... you." I see him in a new light. "I've never done that with anything."

"It's just a coffee shop," he mutters, ducking his head from my scrutiny.

"It's not, it's the cornerstone of Battle Harbour," I echo Leodie's words. "I could go anywhere in Laandia, but I come here. Over and over again. There's a good reason for that."

"I thought it was because of me." Silas's eyes widen as if he can't believe he had just said that. "Because you like my pumpkin spice lattes."

"I do like your lattes," I muse. "But it's more. What you've created is impressive."

"Thanks," he says.

SILAS

F ENELLA HAS BEEN WORKING for almost two hours and it's gone... well.

Better than expected.

If anyone had told me Fenella Carrington would be the newest employee of Coffee for the Sole, I would have laughed and laughed and laughed. But she's still here.

Still smiling, even though I can tell her feet hurt.

Leodie hasn't let her out of her sight, going so far as to forgo her break to make sure Fenella gets the training she needs. It might be because I trained Nathalia and she doesn't trust my methods.

They do seem to be enjoying each other's company, with Jem bustling over like a lost puppy whenever a burst of laughter erupts.

I admit, I feel a little left out when that happens, but so far, Fenella hasn't been too much of a distraction.

I watch Fenella work the cash register as Leodie makes three tea lattes with vanilla and honey for Mrs. Graves and her book club. The group of ladies come in on Thursdays, supposedly to talk about their latest reads, but I think they gossip more than anything.

The way their gray heads are bent together convinces me that the sight of Fenella behind the counter will be the highlight of today's meeting.

There are a lot of good people in Battle Harbour but all of them like to know what's going on, especially Mrs. Graves' book club.

"Well, hello there." Jonathan McKibbon is next in line. From the look on his face, I think he might want to know more about Fenella than the ladies do. "And who might you be?" He looks Fenella up and down and then glances at me off to the side.

I've never been very friendly with Jonathan—he's been a close friend of Prince Kalle since they were boys and they're a few years older than me—but I've always felt a pang of empathy for him. Being friends with a prince would be trying at times. Always a bit behind, never getting the same attention, never quite measuring up.

I wonder if that's the same for Fenella's friends.

"I'm Fenella," she says with a polite smile.

"And I am Sergent Jonathan McKibbon." Do all police officers puff up when they introduce themselves or is it just Jonathan? "I thought today's news was going to be all about Coy Schmidt's car finally moving off his front yard, but I can see it's all about what you're hiding in here, Silas." He grins at Fenella, all toothpaste-white toothy.

I step up to the counter. "I'm not hiding anything. Fenella's agreed to help out while she's in town, or until I find a replacement for Nathalia," I tell him. My tone is pleasant, but I grind my molars at how Jonathan looks at Fenella.

Not that I'm jealous, but... he shouldn't look at her like that. Like she's a fresh treat from the bakery he can't wait to sink his teeth into.

"Wait a sec—Fenella?" Jonathan thumps a hand on the counter. "As in Gunnar's Fenella?"

"As in my own Fenella," she says tightly. "Gunnar and I were a long time ago. And the car is mine." Her shoulders relax when she turns to me. "At least it will be when I get over there to pay him for it?"

"You haven't paid Coy for the car?"

"He said I was good for it. He wanted cash. I need to stop at the bank, but—" She gives me an impish smile. "Working girl now."

"She's working here? *Here*?" Jonathan cuts in.

I meet Fenella's gaze and any reservations I may have had about her working here fly right out the window. "She is."

"To pay for the car? That's a mighty big machine for a little thing like you," he scoffs.

Leodie makes a whistling sound as she sucks in her breath.

The little moment between Fenella and me ends as she turns her head ever so slowly back to stare at Jonathan. I wonder if he feels the cold dread in his belly that I would if Fenella looked at *me* like that.

"Maybe it's too much for a little thing like *you*, but I can handle it just fine," she says and smiles, as insincere as I've ever seen her. "Now, can I help you with something today?"

"Ah, Fenella, I don't think I should say aloud what you could help me with." Despite everything, Jonathan continues with his leering smile. "But maybe I can do something for you." He slides a card across the counter to her. "In case you need help with what's under your hood."

I start to suggest Jonathan watch his mouth but Fenella—

"I wasn't aware the Laandian Police Department makes a habit of inappropriate remarks and innuendos toward their citizens and guests when their officers are on duty." The smile is gone and her eyes spark like amethysts under the light. "I'll be sure to bring that up to King Magnus when I next see him."

"I never—what?" Jonathan blusters, his bravado vanishing at the sight of a strong woman who can clearly take care of herself.

"What can I get you this afternoon, Officer?" Fenella repeats in a sugary sweet voice that's as fake as a package of Splenda.

"Americano, two sugars," I tell her, gently shouldering her away from the cash register. "Why don't you get that for him? I don't think you've made one of those yet today."

Jonathan pays for his coffee without another word to Fenella and mumbles a thank-you when I hand him the cup.

"Have a great day," Fenella calls after him.

"That was Jonathan," I say unnecessarily as he heads out of the door.

"Officer Jonathan." Fenella wipes up the droplets of coffee he spilled. "One of Battle Harbour's finest?"

"Yeah, well... I apologize for him. He's a friend of Kalle's and has always thought he was a bit too big for his britches."

"*You* shouldn't have to apologize for anything. Besides, I can handle little men like that." There is no one in line, and Fenella leans her hip against the counter close enough for me to notice how thick her eyelashes are. It's a strange thing to notice, but it's better than staring at her mouth and the fresh coat of glossy plum she's applied. "Not a friend of yours?"

"I never ran with the royal crowd."

She holds up the business card Jonathan passed her. "It might be handy if I get pulled over for speeding, but that's about it. Not my type," she says matter-of-factly as she tosses the card into the garbage.

"Not upstanding citizens? You go for more of the rock star type?"

"Tiger." Fenella blows a raspberry. "That was not a good type for me."

"So if the rock star isn't your type..." I trail off, wondering what the heck I'm doing. Am I really asking Fenella what her type is? Am I really doing that?

"What type of guy do you like?" Thank god for Leodie. "Because Jonathan is considered a catch in Battle Harbour. Not for me," Leodie quickly adds. "But for a lot of girls in town."

"I think I would throw him back," Fenella says in a prim voice. "If he's a catch? Fish? This is a fishing village," she demands when neither of us reacts. "C'mon."

I groan and Fenella laughs. "I've never really had a type," she admits. "Considering it never works out with the guys I've been hanging around with, you'd think I should try someone different. Don't you?" She looks at me.

"Don't I what?"

"Think I should try someone different, not the selfish, egotistical type like Tiger. And that's not a rock star thing—it's just a him thing. I think I should have *considerate* at the top of my list now. Kind." She drops her voice. "I think *kind* can be very sexy."

"Nice guys are the best," Leodie agrees. "A good cinnamon roll hero."

"I don't know what that is but it sounds delicious."

"You know," Leodie says. "In books or rom-com movies where the guy is good, and sweet and caring. A decent guy. Often goes along with friends falling in love because the girl finally sees what a great person he is." She elbows me. "Like Silas here. Prime example."

I swallow at the way Fenella studies me. "I can see that. Sweet on the outside, but even softer in the middle. I like the description."

If that's so, does that mean she considers me *delicious?*

Fenella

I WORK FOR *FOUR hours*.

It's not that I've never worked for that long before—photoshoots can go for eight hours, and once, shooting a video, I was there for fourteen hours.

This was four hours of dealing with people—customers—and doing things for them and being nice. I can be nice with the best of them, but I learned that even in a place like Laandia, there are quite a few people who don't deserve my niceness.

Silas doesn't have that problem. He just keeps smiling, keeps asking everyone how their day is, any big plans, and what's going in with their kids/grandkids/dogs.

He knows a little about every single person who comes in.

It might be a small-town thing or it might be a Silas thing. Leodie is great. but she doesn't interact half as much as Silas does.

I keep finding new things I like about Silas. First, it was his coffee, then it was his cuteness. Now he's just... *nice*.

It's not a word I like to use, but it fits Silas perfectly.

It fits him like those jeans fit him. That's one more item on the list of things I like about him.

He tells me to leave with enough time to go to the bank before it closes, and I walk out of the shop with tired and aching feet and a promise to come back tomorrow after I take Edie shopping.

It takes a few minutes and a phone call to my business manager to get access to the money for Coy. I don't want to know why he wants cash for the car rather than a more convenient electronic transfer, but whatever works.

I take the money directly to his house so the car can finally be mine.

"Coy's out on the boat," Laura tells me when she greets me at the door. "He'll be gone until late tonight."

"But I told him I'd drop off the money for the car."

"He's not fussed, figures you're good for it," she chuckles. "Plus, he's so over the moon at the car going to a good home. I hope you like it, but I hate the thing. I'd rather have had a new countertop than him spend the money on something like that. Men and their mid-life crisis." She shakes her head. "Now, c'mon in with you. I've something for your supper."

"I don't..." I have no choice but to follow the older woman into the house. Like yesterday, the kitchen is full of amazing smells, with a pot bubbling on the stove.

"Lobster chowder." Laura gives the pot a stir before turning it down. "I'll put it in a thermos for you. I know Lottie Merman at the castle kitchen, and she can't make a chowder to save her life. Not like mine."

"You don't have to feed me," I protest, feeling unsettled at how Laura has pulled me into the warmth of her home, and how it sets off a glow inside me.

Laura gives me a sharp glance. "Someone better start." I laugh; in all my years of modelling, no one has ever suggested I need *more* food for my frame. "What does your mother think of this?"

"About me? Not much, if she can help it," I say. "We're not close."

"Shame, bright girl like you. Buys her own car. Doesn't wait for a man to get it for her." Laura frowns as she ladles soup into a giant thermos. "What does your mother do?"

"She lunches with her friends. And she likes martinis. Other than that—" I lift a shoulder. I've had four hours in Coffee for the Sole, answering all types of questions, so Laura asking about my mother shouldn't surprise me. "I honestly have no idea. We're really not close. She prefers my brother. Both of them."

"Pity. I wasn't blessed with a daughter, but I would have loved a girl. Better than those lazy layabouts for sons I've got. And the daughters-in-law they give me." She raises her eyes to the ceiling. "A McKibbon and a Crow. What am I supposed to do with that?"

I struggle to follow along because Laura's accent is strong, like a mix of Irish, Scottish and Canadian, and because I have no idea who she's talking about. My guess is that her sons married women from not-great families in town, but I don't feel I should ask for details.

"McKibbon." I do recognize that name. "He's the police?"

Laura rolls her eyes. "Thinks he's better'en the rest of us because he's friendly with the prince. If you ask me, and you should, Kate is the only good one of that lot. Now, she's done something with her life."

"I think I met her. Kate works for the royal family?"

"Yes. Good girl."

I'm not sure if Laura means me or Kate, but I take the compliment for myself.

"Now, here." Laura screws on the top of the thermos. "This is good chowder. You eat it all." She pushes it at me.

"Ah... thank you?" The silver container is warm to the touch and my mouth is already watering just from the smell alone. "I can bring this back tomorrow."

"Keep it, Coy's got enough. He fills them up, takes them on the boat. Or bring it back if you want me to fill it up again."

"I think I'll bring it back," I say, giving her a hesitant smile.

Laura's answering smile is warm and genuine. "You do that."

Business completed, I take my gift of lobster chowder out to the car and wonder what I should do to keep myself busy. Gunnar told me about his meeting tonight, and I can tell Stella's not entirely comfortable with me yet. I could see what Sophie was doing or—

What time does the coffee shop close?

It closes at the exact time I pull up in front of it. I honk when I see Silas flipping the old-fashioned Open sign in the window over to Closed, and he comes out.

"You're back." Silas leans against the open window, his smile also warm and genuine. It adds to the glow that seems to be burning bright inside me.

"And you haven't left."

"Duty calls. As you can see, I'm closing up for the night. What are you up to?"

"It seems to me that there might be a common misunderstanding that my car is too much car for me," I tell.

"That was just Jonathan—"

"I can prove myself and give you a ride," I interrupt. "Somewhere. Just so you can vouch for me being a capable driver."

"Fenella, you don't need anyone to vouch for you."

"But I'd like to go for a drive," I say, suddenly unsure. Me, who has held conversations with A-listers everywhere, who once approached Leo DiCaprio to ask him for dinner, and went up to Tom Holland at some awards show and invited him for a drink. This was before Zendaya, of course.

So why is the Fenella who did all that having trouble asking Silas to go for a drive with her?

"With you," I finish in a rush. "If you're not busy. Or have plans. Or a date."

Silas's smile slowly creeps across his face like the sun rising in the morning. "You heard Wyatt—I don't date. And my plans involve staying awake to get another glimpse at Neptune tonight."

"I can help with that." I grab the thermos from the passenger seat. "I have soup."

"Soup. Well, then." He straightens up and gives a tap. "I'll get us a couple of coffees and lock up. Be right out."

"I'll be here," I tell him, the warm glow shooting off fireworks inside me now.

SILAS

"**H**I," FENELLA SAYS AS I slide into her car. Her smile is a mix of excitement and uncertainty, and the combination is adorable.

I never would have imagined Fenella could be adorable. There is a thesaurus-length worth of descriptives for her, but adorable? Cute?

Seeing her behind the wheel of a bright yellow Charger, with the engine rumbling like a low-grade earthquake? Definitely cute.

I hand her a cup. "Pumpkin spice and vanilla."

Her fingers brush mine as she takes it. "You remembered."

"It's not that difficult, since you had three of them already today. Maybe I should have made it a decaf."

She shakes her head as she takes a sip. "Caffeine does nothing to me. I think it was all the Red Bulls I drank when I was younger."

"That stuff will rot your stomach."

"Don't tell my brother or Gunnar. The company sponsored them for a while when they were playing at extreme sports."

"That shouldn't be something you *play* with." I take a sip of my tea—caffeine does do things for me, so I've switched to decaffeinated Earl Grey with steamed milk—and study Fenella. "What's the plan?"

"I don't do plans." She laughs. "Haven't you figured that out yet?"

"There are quite a few things I've yet to figure out about you," I tell her honestly.

"I'm a woman of mystery. Actually, I'm not. My life is an open book to all. You said I should see more of Laandia." Taking another sip of her coffee, she settles the cup in the holder in the console between the seats. Her phone is propped up, playing the latest Taylor Swift album.

This should be uncomfortable; I barely know Fenella. She now works for me—sort of, since she refuses to let me pay her—but what do I really know about her?

I know she smells like cherries. That she favours silver jewelry, especially her collection of rings. And that her selection of coats will not be warm enough for October in Laandia. "And you should see more of it. Is that what you had in mind? Sightseeing in the dark?"

"Maybe some stars?"

The fact that she asks does strange things to my insides. "Sounds good to me."

"Where should we go then?"

"Seems like you're in the driver's seat."

"Buckle up, baby." Fenella shifts into gear and pulls away with a satisfying roar of the engine. "You have a lot of faith in me, considering I was the one who was lost last night," she points out as she does a loop around the town square.

"Were you really lost, or just curious? Turn down this street."

From the flash of her eyes, I see I was right, and I chuckle softly. "Where did the soup come from?"

"Lobster chowder from Laura Schmidt. In case you're hungry."

"Nice. A full-service kidnapping. Turn right."

"How can it be a kidnapping if you came willingly? And are giving me directions?"

"You lured me with soup and a shiny car."

"Is that all it takes? You've got to work on your standards, Silas." Fenella grins at me. I've spent the day watching her smiles and this is another new one. Mischievous. Impulsive?

And—intimate? That's what it feels like, being caught in a bubble of new-car smell and Taylor singing about being forgotten.

"How come the car still smells new?" I wonder as I direct Fenella to the road south of town that hugs the coast. The moon hangs low in the sky behind us and I can already see the twinkle of Venus along the horizon.

Fenella pats the dashboard with a possessive smile. "I've no idea, because it's not new. But it's clean. Maybe Coy uses some special cleaning stuff."

"That doesn't sound like Coy."

She glances over at me. "Maybe it's magic."

"Do you believe in magic, Fenella?"

She shakes her head. "I'd like to, but no. I have a good life, but I know none of it is because of magic."

"Oh, I don't know, I've seen some of your makeup videos. That's a kind of magic, isn't it?"

Fenella gives a peal of embarrassed laughter. "Oh, my god, you've watched them?"

"Wyatt. He's obsessed. I'd be worried, but I know he's harmless. Do you know you have a Wikipedia page?"

"I do? Weird."

Fenella drives as fast as I expected but has full control of the car, shifting gears like a pro and taking the curves in the road like she grew up driving them. I revise my earlier *cute* impression because the way she drives this car is kind of hot.

I make a mental note to tell Wyatt so he can add to his Fenella collection of facts, but think better of it. He doesn't need the encouragement.

Waves crash against the shore on one side, towering trees with colourful leaves muted in the dim light line the other. The car's headlights illuminate ahead of us. I've always loved the loneliness of this road.

It's just Fenella and me in her new, old car.

I never would have expected this when she walked into the shop a few days ago. Or when I first saw her with Gunnar years ago.

Or when Wyatt showed me that handbag ad with its millions of views.

I'm alone with Fenella Carrington, and I better make the most of it.

I point to her phone as the song changes. "Favourite song?"

"Off an album or of all time?"

"Off the album."

"Are you a Swiftie?"

"Actually, no. But it's a way to get to know my latest employee."

"You want to get to know me because I'm your employee?"

"Sure. I'm a good boss."

Fenella chuckles. "Okay, then. I'll go with Smallest Man Alive because it reminds me of Tiger."

"He really messed you up, didn't he?"

She takes a moment before answering. "He really didn't. It wasn't enjoyable to catch him cheating on me, but I'm almost as mad at how I reacted as at what he did, and that shows that I didn't care *all* that much."

"Very mature of you."

"I have my moments. Why aren't you dating anyone?" She glances over to gauge my reaction. "Just getting to know my boss," she says cheerfully.

I take a moment before I answer. This isn't like Stella or Sophie, or even Edie, with their constant questions about my lack of dating life. Or Wyatt bugging me. This is me alone in a car with Fenella, and since it's probably going to be a once-in-a-lifetime occurrence, why not be honest?

"I guess it's because someone messed me up," I confess. "It took me a while to get over it, and I didn't want to start anything until I was sure."

"Why did she leave? Small town," she adds. "People talk."

"Edie or Leodie?" I guess. "Or Sophie."

"Possibly all of the above."

I chuckle. "Mia." Her name doesn't completely eradicate my good mood, so that's a start. "If you didn't get her name."

"It's more important to find out what she did and why," Fenella says. "I can make up some good names after that."

"She left... she left because she didn't want the life I offered her," I admit. Saying her name is one thing, rehashing her reasons is another. "The life I wanted wasn't enough for her. I wasn't good enough for her."

My words hang between us, lit by the dim light of the dashboard.

I probably shouldn't have admitted that.

"I don't see it that way," Fenella says quickly, too quickly for the thought to have just popped into her mind. The way people talk about my relationship with Mia shows how everyone has an opinion. Everyone has a way it could have been fixed, salvaged, saved.

Ask anyone in town, and they have an opinion on what went wrong with Mia and me, even if they don't know the details.

For the first time, I realize Fenella and I have more in common than I would have thought.

"And how do you see it?" I ask stiffly.

"You say she didn't want what you were offering, which I guess would be safety and security. A comfortable life, with family and friends."

I can't help but cringe at her explanation. "You make it sound extremely boring."

"Not for some."

"For you?"

Fenella pauses, mulling over the question like she's got a new flavour of candy in her mouth. "I have financial security, but that's it," she begins. "I've never been in a long-term, committed relationship, but if I was, and it wasn't the right guy, I could see feeling like I was trapped."

Trapped? "So you're saying I wasn't the right guy for her."

"That's obvious." She glances over at me. "You probably don't want to hear this, but I think she made the right decision to leave. She wanted a different kind of life, and if she'd stayed—and I'm sure that was the easier decision because you're amazing—if she'd stayed, she'd have ended up resenting you. I don't believe in regretting things, but in my opinion, she'd have ended up regretting not leaving. And if you had a marriage and kids, that just gets messy."

Messy. Isn't that what Mia told me—she wanted a clean break?

"Sorry if I hit a nerve," she adds softly.

"I think all my nerves about this were cauterized years ago," I tell her ruefully.

"Ew. That sounds painful."

"It was. But not so much anymore."

I've spent years hiding my feelings and telling everyone I was fine. Mia leaving did mess me up—not only was it the ending of a real, serious relationship but I lost my best friend.

I wasn't what Mia wanted, and for years, I've thought it was my fault. That I was lacking.

But maybe it wasn't all me. Maybe she was missing something. Maybe she wouldn't have been able to give me what she wanted and leaving really was the best for us both.

Maybe. The word looms ahead of me like the empty road, opening up so many possibilities.

"Turn left after the next curve," I instruct Fenella.

"Ah. You do have a plan," she says as she slows down for the curve—not enough, but at least we don't take the turn on two wheels.

"Not really, but I have ideas," I admit.

"Ideas are always good."

"Sometimes. So you think I'm amazing, do you?"

Fenella

I DON'T ANSWER THAT.

I laugh, but I don't admit that I think he's amazing. That the more time I spend with Silas Bell, the more I want to know about him. What makes him so decent and kind? What are his favourite things, and how can I make sure he gets them?

And why in the world hasn't some woman snatched him up?

What kind of woman would he want to snatch him up?

"Where are you taking me?" I ask instead as I turn onto a road that's even more deserted than the one we were following.

"There's, uh, sort of a park along the water. Just here. Pull over here."

I do as he asks, pulling the car to the side of the road and tucking it under the trees. The spot doesn't seem like any sort of park that I've ever visited. There's a clearing near the water, but nothing is there but a bench. Like the area near the lighthouse, the ground is made up of huge rocks jutting over the ocean.

"This is a sort of park?" I ask as I idle the engine.

"Sort of. It's a bench." He huffs in indecision. "There was an older couple who used to live around here, and they would come here to look at the stars. When she died, he built a bench here."

"Is this older couple your grandparents?" I wonder.

"Great-aunt and uncle. He's the one who taught me about the stars," Silas confesses.

And he brought me to this spot that is obviously special for him. Warmth floods me as I turn off the car. "It's a perfect spot for our picnic." I reach into the back for the thermos. "Or for eating the chowder."

The car clicks as the engine cools. A cold breeze rustles the leaves on the ground and those remaining on the branches above. It's dark, deserted, and might be slightly spooky if Silas hadn't grabbed my hand as I was about to walk across the road without checking.

"Look both ways," he warns. "Cars do come along here."

"I'll believe it when I see it."

Silas's hands are large and weathered, with long fingers and neatly clipped nails. I can't help but think of how I used to marvel at Tiger's hands, with his calluses from playing guitar and his black-painted nails. They were the hands of a boy playing at being a rock star.

Silas doesn't have to play at anything. He's a man; a good man.

Still holding my hand, Silas leads me across the road and along the path to the bench. The wind is stronger, blowing off the ocean, and colder. I shiver into my pink puffer jacket—warmer than the one I wore last night, but not nearly enough protection.

"Do you have a blanket in the car?" Silas asks.

"I have nothing in the car."

He holds out his hand. "Keys. I'll check the trunk. Keep away from the edge," he warns as he takes the keys from me and heads back to the car.

I stop at the bench in the middle of nowhere and look out to the water. Waves crash incessantly with an almost hypnotic rhythm.

There are whales out there. Icebergs. Boats, like Coy in his fishing trawler.

I can't see a thing in the dark except the odd whitecap breaking over the water.

It's not until I sit down that I look up.

"Wow," I breathe.

Pinpricks of light dot the sky, which is a rainbow of shades of mauve and purple reaching to the indigo straight above me. I tilt my head back and take it all in.

"A lot of stars," Silas says from behind me.

"Uh-huh. Beautiful."

"Uh-huh." He clears his throat. "I found this." He has a wool blanket in his hands. "Coy left his emergency pack in the trunk."

"That was nice of him. How did you know there'd be something there?" I ask as Silas drops the blanket on my lap.

"Around here, everyone has something in their trunk." He joins me on the bench, the heat of his body making my right side toasty warm.

"Do you think we'll see more shooting stars?"

"Maybe." He clears his throat and moves just a little closer, so his thigh rests against mine. "But the Draconid meteor shower is due to start in a week or so."

"Meteors? Aren't they what crash into the oceans and cause giant tidal waves that destroy the world?"

"Big ones, sure, but I like to hope that's only going to happen in the movies."

I point to the water. "Because if it was real, then Laandia would be gone."

"Probably. And I like it here."

"So do I."

And I do. In the last two days, Battle Harbour has gone from a boring little town where Gunnar lives and not much happens, to a place where I like to spend time.

I'm enjoying myself here, not simply hiding out and planning my next move, and hoping time flies by.

I don't remember the last time I just *sat*. Not talking, not looking at my phone, just being still. I can't even meditate when I'm home, so this should be painful for me.

Only it's not.

"It's so peaceful," I tell him, still staring above.

He hums. "I like peaceful."

"I never thought I did, but I like this."

We sit in silence for a long moment, but it's not awkward or uncomfortable. We just *sit*, breathing in the cool air, admiring the beauty of the spot.

"No taking pictures?" he asks.

I shake my head. This is different than last night—more solitary. It's not only that my latest posts got more traffic than I expected, and that there may be a 'Find Fenella' game on TikTok, much like Pokémon Go, but for once, I don't need to have video evidence of everywhere I go.

"Don't you take pictures?" I ask.

"Sometimes." Silas tilts his head back and I let my gaze skim the column of his throat. "But I find that people are too concerned with taking the perfect picture and miss out on so much. I think forgetting about the phone or the camera means you take in more. Enjoy it more. Experience it fully so you can have that memory, not just a picture on your camera reel that you may never look at again."

I just want to enjoy this moment. Experience it. And no one needs my memory of it.

Silas is solid beside me, my shoulder resting against his arm, his thigh pressing lightly against mine. His coffee/pine/sweet-something scent surrounds me, making me think it might be nice to get a little closer to him. Not just for warmth but because he smells really good.

What would happen if I slid onto his lap? Rested my head against his chest? Twined my fingers in his wavy hair, teasing the curls at the back of his neck. Moving my mouth close enough to touch my lips against his.

The image hits me like a wave crashing against the rocks below.

What would happen if I acted on it?

What could happen is that he might be surprised enough that he'd dump me in the water by accident, so I best not try any of the above. Silas gives me the impression that he moves at a slower pace than I'm used to, so I check my speed.

"We should have chowder," I decide. "Only... I don't have a spoon."

"Well, that's a shame." He takes the thermos from me. "But this here is a cup, so we're good. It is soup, after all." As Silas carefully opens the silver container and pours a cupful, I spread the blanket across our laps, careful not to knock his arm.

Not to touch him at all because I'm afraid if I do, I'll forget about surprising him and give in to the urge and crawl right onto his lap.

I've never stopped myself from acting on my attraction to a man.

If I meet someone and there's a connection, I act on it. I don't wait for him to call or make the first move. There's no wondering if he'll kiss me tonight or wait for the next date.

I'm a go-getter. If I see someone I want, I go get him. It's how every single one of my relationships has begun—me taking initiative.

I'm not going to do this with Silas because I don't think me making the first move on this new attraction is the right thing to do.

This attraction isn't exactly new—if I'm being honest, I've been secretly interested in Silas since the first time he handed me my pumpkin spice latte, with the hearts etched on the foam. I just never imagined ever being in the position to do anything about it. We're from different worlds. Small town, big city. He drives a solid, staid Corolla and I race around in my flashy yellow Charger.

That says it right there.

But when Silas hands me the cup of chowder, steam rising and the scent of cream and butter and lobster making my mouth water, something inside me says that maybe sliding into his world might not be the worst thing.

"Thank you," I say, brushing my fingers against his as I take the cup. I blow on the soup before I take a sip and then— "Oh. Wow." Rich, creamy broth flavoured with lobster. Chunks of lobster meat. "This is so good." I moan, taking an even bigger mouthful.

"Smells good."

"I'm going to eat it all unless you stop me," I warn.

"Take as much as you like. I'll just sit and listen to the sounds of your appreciation."

It sounds... interesting... the way he says that. And then I take another mouthful and moan again.

Oh.

"Do you come here often?" I ask to take my mind off everything else it's thinking.

"Not really. I've come a few times by myself, brought Wyatt a couple more."

"What's the best thing about living here?"

"The water," he says. "When I went to school, I couldn't hear the waves and it took me forever to fall asleep. The sound, and the movement... it's like a part of me."

"So you have to live here forever."

"No, I just need to be near water. Preferably the ocean." He glances over. "Where do *you* live? I don't even know that."

"I'm 'from away' as everyone calls it. That's all you need to know."

"I'd like to know more."

The sincerity in his tone twists my stomach in a good way. Trying to tell my heart to quit with the high-speed pitter-patter, I finish the chowder and hand the cup back to Silas. "Your turn. My father has houses in Los Angeles, London, and an apartment in Tokyo," I begin. "There's another apartment in New York and a place in St. Lucia. I live in any number of those places, depending on what I've got going on, unless I'm staying with one of my friends."

"Your friends are—"

"The Billionaire Brats. You can call us that. Unlike the Brat Pack of the 1980s, we don't take offence."

"You don't seem too bratty," he muses, holding the cup of chowder up and breathing in the smell.

"Tell that to my mother. No—" I make a cutting motion with my hand. "I am not about to ruin a perfectly nice evening with thoughts of her."

I hold my breath as Silas sips, expecting him to pepper me with questions about my parents. But he doesn't.

"You mentioned in the car that you refuse to regret anything. What if you did?" Silas asks. "What would you regret?"

"Never falling in love," I say without giving it any thought.

"You've never been in love?" he asks with surprise. "But you've been engaged..."

"Unfortunately," I agree. "And maybe I thought I was in love at the time, but looking back, I'm not sure. What I felt for them wasn't what I thought love feels like."

"What do you think love feels like?"

I have to think about that for a moment; a long moment, enough for Silas to finish the cup and offer me more. I ask for half a cup.

"This," I finally admit in a low voice. "Not—*this*." I gesture between us with the cup. "But being comfortable. Being able to be myself with someone. I always felt I had to be the person they wanted me to be. Not me."

"Are you able to be just you very often?"

"Not really, no. I think that's why I like it here. I'm just able to be *me*, and no one is judging me, or laughing behind my back, or trying to win me over because they want something from me."

Just saying that makes me feel sad.

I nudge Silas with my shoulder. "You're not allowed to ask all the questions. What do you like about living here?"

He takes a deep breath. Is that a slight lean towards me, or is it in my head? "The community. Obviously not everyone, but I like that we're all in this together. We get through the storms together, we get to have a really cool king. We care about each other, there's always support. It's like family, but more."

"I've never had that before," I tell him wistfully. "I have my friends and I love them, but other people aren't that supportive. It's different here. Meeting Sophie and Leodie, even Laura—it makes me feel good. Being here makes me feel good—when I'm not feeling left out because I don't have my own community."

"This can be your community," Silas assures me. "When you're here."

I can hear the unspoken question in his voice. *How long will you be here?*

I don't want him to ask out loud because I don't know the answer.

"What's that star?" I ask to fill the silence. I point to a bright light in the sky.

Silas takes the cup and refills it for himself. "That might be the International Space Station," he says with a chuckle. "But that one—" —he moves my hand— "—is Aldebaran, part of the Taurus constellation."

"The Bull. I'm a Scorpio myself."

"I might have been able to guess that, if I followed that sort of thing."

"Stars, but not horoscopes. Got it."

Silas finishes the soup and sets the thermos on the ground before us. I adjust the blanket and we sit quietly for a long time, looking up.

"Why did you hire me?" I ask finally.

"I thought you'd be fun," Silas says softly.

"And what do you think now?"

"I suspect you might be more fun than I can handle. You did kidnap me, after all."

I smile with cold lips. "I persuaded you with lobster chowder. There's a difference."

SILAS

I WOULD REALLY LIKE to kiss Fenella.

Like, really *really* want to kiss her.

But the little voice inside puts a stop to any moves I might still have. Not *she's not going to kiss you back*, because I'm fairly certain Fenella would be very into kissing me back. But the one that keeps repeating—*she's leaving*.

"What would you be doing if you were home?" I ask to torture myself.

Fenella starts like she was deep in her own thoughts. "Do you know why I'm here?"

"Laandia is a great place to visit?" She smiles and I continue. "I thought it had something to do with the video of you throwing a fairly substantial ring at your fiancé."

"Ex-fiancé, just so we're clear. He's very ex."

Good to know.

"My father suggested I stay out of sight until it all blows over," Fenella continues. "His suggestion was more of an order than a request. I've been wanting to work for the company for a few years, and I thought he was going to make that happen, but then Tiger happened. Public embarrassment and no job."

"That's..." All I can think of is that's what she's got waiting for her at home. Not a man, not friends who will be more fun, more entertaining than I could ever be, but a job.

And I've already figured out that it's important for Fenella to prove herself.

"Yeah. It's that," she says heavily. "I've been basically exiled here. Not that it's a bad place to be exiled. Gunnar offered a room in the castle, and I didn't even think of going anywhere else."

"I think it's great that the two of you are such good friends still."

"It really is," she agrees. "And thankfully Stella isn't one to get jealous. I had a boyfriend who hated the fact I had male friends. Super red flag there. He didn't last long."

"How did you meet Gunnar?"

"Through my brother, when they were both racing for Red Bull. That's an awful lot of questions you're trying to fit in there, you know."

"I thought I'd update your Wikipedia page while you're here," I joke. Fenella laughs loud enough to disrupt something in the bush to the side. "Seriously, though, I think you're interesting." That didn't come out too awkward.

It might have had I admitted that I find her fascinating.

"Well, I think you're interesting too." She meets my gaze, holds it for a long moment until I drop my chin.

"I own a coffee shop and look at stars. I don't even have a cat," I tell her ruefully.

"Do cats make you interesting?"

"Of course, they're basically the devil incarnate. It takes a certain type of person to survive their evil wiles."

"Are we talking about the same cats? Cute, furry, little toe beans on their paws? Or do you mean the naked cats, because yes, I'll give you that. They are evil."

I laugh.

I can't kiss her. As much as I want to, I'm not going to, because it will ruin this wonderful bubble we've created. This friendship, the magic, whatever else I can call what's developed between us.

Even if I kiss her, she's still going to leave, and I don't want it to be more difficult than it's going to be.

"I'm really good at the dating part," she admits like she can read my mind. "It's the relationships that I get mucked up on."

"What was your longest relationship?" I ask. "Or is that too much to ask?"

"No, that's something you'd ask your friend," she teases. "Not my friends, because they'd already know everything about it, thanks to pictures and social media posts about it. My longest was actually Gunnar. Six months."

"But you were engaged?"

"Twice. Both were spur-of-the-moment things—I only knew Lennon for a couple of days. We met at Paris Fashion Week when we were modelling for Gucci. Lennon Gallagher?"

I shake my head. "Have you heard of Oasis? Big in the 90s? That's his dad's band. It annoys me when everyone thinks Millie Bobby Brown is so cool for being with Jon Bon Jovi's son, and they all forget I had a rocker's son first."

My ego, which had shrivelled slightly after last night, now tucks itself up and into my pocket at the name-dropping Fenella does. There is no way I can kiss her now.

No way.

But still, I trudge forward because this is what you do with friends. "And the second time was with... Tiger?"

Fenella rolls her eyes. "Worst mistake ever. Actually, I dated a hockey player once—he who shall not be named—and that was an even bigger mistake. No more hockey players. No more musicians, either. Lennon played in a band too."

"Maybe you should just stay away from famous men," I suggest.

"Yeah." The way she looks at me... "Maybe."

We stay on the bench for a while longer. I point out stars as they appear, we ask each other questions about our lives.

There's not much we have in common, but it's fun. I'm having fun. Fenella laughs a lot.

I don't kiss her.

"What you said to Wyatt last night," I say instead. "I assume you were talking about yourself."

She rolls her eyes. "No, my twin brother."

"Really? But you—"

"Yes, it was about me. But I don't mention my relationship with my mother as a rule, except if I'm paying three hundred dollars and lying on a therapist's couch."

"Therapy is a good thing."

"You don't sound convinced."

"My mother thinks we should get Wyatt to talk to someone," I tell her.

"Because he's gay or because he has mother issues."

"He's handling the gay thing really well. He came out when he was eleven to his best friend while they were playing video games. Wyatt told me he seemed unimpressed but beat him in Fortnite so things went well."

She frowns. "As opposed to Wyatt beating him?"

"His way of thinking was that if Jack had issues with him, he would have let Wyatt win or not played against him at all. I can't say I understand his logic."

"As long as it makes sense to him. I've never understood the draw of Fortnite either."

"You've played?"

"Twin brother, remember? I bet you're a gamer."

"Board games, actually."

"You should have board games in your coffee shop. Bring in the non-coffee crowd."

"That's... a good idea."

"I know. Don't sound so surprised. You should know by now that I'm full of them."

Fenella laughs. I like the way it sounds. I like hearing it. Her straight-out belly laugh is contagious.

Sometimes I forget to laugh with her because I'm smiling at her so much.

"I probably shouldn't have said anything about Wyatt," I muse.

"I let it slip that my mother values her handbag more than me, so we're fair. I don't mention my mother to anyone, but listening to how Wyatt sounds so hung up about an absent mother who never should have gotten pregnant in the first place— Sorry," she checks herself. "That's your sister."

"It is."

"I'm sure that is pretty tough for a sixteen-year-old to deal with, but the kid seems to have everything else going for him. I like him."

"I'll be sure to tell him. Like I said, he's your biggest fan."

Eventually, I wrap Fenella in the blanket and tuck her under my arm, but I can still feel her shivers.

She's so cold, but she's just as reluctant as I am to end tonight.

Eventually, I make the call and we head back to the car. The heat goes on full blast, but she keeps the music quiet.

"You need a warmer coat," I say after her teeth have stopped chattering and we're almost back to town.

"It's first on my list. I'll have to give Coy back his blanket."

"I wouldn't bother. You might need it again."

"Does this mean we can do this again?"

The hope in her voice makes my heart stutter; seriously stutter like it needs a kickstart. But I keep my voice even like she didn't just rock my world with a simple question. "You want to work for me, *and* hang out? That's a lot of me," I warn her.

"I think I can handle it," she says with all the confidence of knowing what she wants.

Or maybe it's knowing she can have what she wants.

I'm not sure that's going to work out for me.

All too soon, Fenella pulls up in front of the shop. "I had no idea you lived next door," she says, staring at the empty storefront next door. "What used to be in there?"

"Flower shop, an attempt at Mexican food, cookies. The latest was an insurance guy."

"I guess I thought you still lived with your parents."

"I'm thirty years old," I tell her ruefully. "I shouldn't be living with my parents. I moved here after the insurance guy bunked off," I add.

"At least you have your own place," she says in a wistful voice.

Is that because I have my own place and she doesn't, or because she'd appreciate the privacy of my own place?

That doesn't help the fact my mind is swinging like a pendulum.

Kiss her.

Run.

Kiss her.

Run.

Instead of doing either, I sit there in the car and try to look anywhere but at Fenella.

"Silas." Fenella puts a hand on my leg.

"You're leaving," I blurt.

"Not yet."

"But you're leaving."

She sighs, and it's as if the air is expelled from my own body. I like this woman. I like her a lot. And it's not the silly infatuation I felt looking at her Instagram posts and TikTok videos. Fenella is surprisingly sweet and funny, and honest. Growing up entitled and in the most luxurious of settings has given her issues, but I'm amazed at how down-to-earth she really is.

Or maybe that's just who she is around me. Here, in Laandia. She would be a totally different person elsewhere, when she needs to show the world everything about her.

I like how she is around me.

But she will leave and I will not.

"Can I still work for you?" Fenella's a smart woman—she knows what's going on, why I'm putting on the brakes.

I'm grateful I don't have to say anything more. "Even if I said no, I don't think you'd listen. You'd show up and start making drinks."

"I like making drinks. Maybe that's my calling."

I can't resist—reaching out, I touch her cheek with the back of my hand. Her skin is soft and still cold. A tendril of her dark hair snags around my finger, soft and silky. "I think your calling will be something much bigger than making drinks," I tell her seriously. "That's why I'm going to say goodnight."

I open the door and slide out of the car.

"Goodnight, Silas," she calls after me, her voice heavy with resignation.

Fenella

I HAVE A HORRIBLE feeling I'm going to break Silas's heart and there's nothing I can do about it.

Or maybe he's going to break mine.

Either way, someone is going to get hurt. The smart thing would be to keep my distance; stop working at the coffee shop. Stop drinking coffee altogether. Forget about star gazing and late nights out in the cold and the look in Silas's green eyes when he said good night.

But I've never been that smart when it comes to men.

I wake up with a surge of excitement that I'll see Silas today.

I meet Edie in Battle Harbour before I go to work, and we run through the stores in record time because she has to be at the pub by noon.

I have to go to work too. I hug that to myself because it feels strange that I'm eager to be at the coffee shop, making lattes and talking with Leodie and catching Silas looking at me out of the corner of my eye, when it's clear from the passive-aggressive comments Edie makes that she clearly wants to do other things than inventory at The King's Hat.

I don't say a word about Silas even when Edie moans about how she didn't take the time to grab a coffee before we met. Even without the caffeine, she flashes through Sara's Sport and Arnold's Attire like she's on a royal mission.

In a way, she is. Edie will be queen one day and she needs to start dressing like it.

I help her with that—making suggestions on colours and styles and what works with her body type and what clearly doesn't. I pick out a week's worth of wardrobe for her, every-day outfits that are *her*, but elevated just a little more. I find four dresses suitable for special occasions and promise to take her to New York to look for more when my exile is over.

I buy a much warmer coat for myself, gloves and a selection of hats. Even if I stay for just one more week, who knows how cold it will get?

"How long are you staying for?" Edie asks as one of the security guards assigned to Prince Kalle takes an armload of bags from her.

Only in Laandia can the future queen spend a morning shopping without an entourage. I take more people to the shops, and I'm just me.

"I'm not sure." The pictures I posted of the sky didn't go viral but they've been shared far and wide with the caption, "Where is heartbroken Fenella hiding out?"

I'm very glad I didn't include any of Silas or Wyatt. The texts I got from my father's assistant were bad enough, asking if I knew the meaning of *under the radar* and *low profile* and overt comments about how the board of Carrington was not pleased with my continual attempts for attention.

I've never liked Assistant Peter.

"I have a favour to ask," Edie says hesitantly as we pause outside Helen's Hunt.

"If it involves shopping, I'm all in."

"A little different, but I think it might help *you* out as well. I know you have your car to make it easier to get into town," she begins, "but what do you think of actually staying in town?"

"Is there a castle around that I haven't noticed?"

"Not a royal place. Mine. How would you feel about house-sitting for me? Cat-sitting, actually."

"You have a cat?"

All I can think of is how Silas thinks he'd be more interesting with a cat. And then the idea of *having my own place* hits me like I've slammed into a tree while speeding along in my car, and I hop with excitement. "You have a house?"

"An apartment. And I have Ernie. Kalle has Bertie, and they do not get along, which is why we haven't integrated them. Bertie won't let Kalle out of her sight, so she's at the castle with us. I had to leave Ernie behind at my place, but he's not handling being alone very well."

"Why do you still have your own place when you're living with Kalle at the castle?" I wonder.

"I haven't figured out who to rent it out to," she admits. "And because there's not a lot of interest in living right beside the pub. It can get kind of loud at night."

"Fair," I say. "I'm loud at night. I mean... that wouldn't bother me."

"It's not the castle," Edie continues, sounding like she's doing her best to dissuade me. "There's no Mrs. Theissen to look after things—"

"Mrs. Theissen terrifies me," I confess.

"Join the club. If you're looking for a change, I'd love if you stayed at my place while you're here to look after my cat." She smiles hopefully.

My eagerness bubbles as much as the steamer at Coffee for the Sole. "I'd love to."

We have just enough time to run over to Edie's apartment. I know even before I step foot inside that I'm going to love staying there. Gunnar is leaving in the next few days for his trip with Stella, and while I've never felt anything but welcome at the castle, it might be strange if he's not there.

It doesn't take long for Edie to show me around. One bedroom, bath, living room/kitchen combo, and a cat. But the idea of staying here excites me.

I've never had a place to myself.

I leave my bags in the bedroom after she hands me the keys. I tell Ernie the cat that I'll see him soon. I don't have time to move my things today, since my shift is about to start and I don't want to be late—for various reasons, none of which are because I'm a punctual person—plus, I've been invited to a family dinner at the castle tonight.

After I say goodbye to Edie and practically skip across the square, I realize that Edie's apartment and Silas's place are directionally kitty-corner from each other.

That makes me even happier.

"How was shopping?" Jem calls as I sweep into the shop. Jem is tall and gangly and looks a bit like a scarecrow. But he seems nice and even more excited than Leodie about me working here.

"It was great," I sing.

Leodie gives me a strange expression. "Shopping in Battle Harbour is never great."

"It was today. Is Silas here?"

Jem points at the wall. "He ran back to his place. Something about needing to check on something."

I'm already backing toward the door. "Have I got a minute? I just have to show him what I got."

I turn to the door even before they answer. "You can show us," Leodie calls after me.

"I will. Back in a minute," I throw over my shoulder. Out one door and in the next—but the door to the empty storefront is locked.

Is there another way in? A door at the back, through the alley like at Edie's?

I take a glance down the narrow walkway.

I'm not going down there. I bang on the door, wait a moment, and then knock louder.

It takes a moment, but Silas eventually appears. "Fenella?" He looks confused as he unlocks the door, with his hair more mussed than usual, like he's run his hands through it. "What's wrong?"

He's wearing another plaid flannel shirt and I think it's my favourite yet. It's the right shade of green with browney-orange lines running through it.

I think it brings out the green in his eyes.

"I need to show you what I got," I tell him, pushing past him into— "You live here?"

The room is long and narrow, half the size of the coffee shop, and covered in a layer of dirt. Thick cobwebs hang in the corners of the ceilings and piles of dried leaves and old newspapers dot the floor.

I whirl around to face Silas. "You live like this?"

"I live upstairs. I use the door at the back. I keep this—" —he glances around— "—closed. Because it's a mess."

"Just a little. What's your place like upstairs?" I ask with a fair amount of concern. If Silas lives like this...

"Much better than here," he assures me, rubbing at the back of his neck. "I haven't been in here in weeks. It's kind of a... yeah. Are you okay? You scared me with your knocking."

"I had to show you what I bought." The state of the store has dimmed some of my enthusiasm for my news, but I quickly get it back, along with a flurry of ideas. "And to tell you I'll be staying in town!"

"You are?" Silas sounds incredulous.

"Edie asked me to house-sit for her while I'm in Laandia," I explain. "She has a cat, and I don't think he's the devil incarnate."

"You're staying at Edie's while you're here." He deflates a little but still gives me an encouraging nod. "That's great. Ernie needs company. And staying at the castle must feel like a big hotel."

"I'm used to staying at big hotels."

"By yourself?"

"Sometimes."

"Sounds lonely."

"I'm never lonely," I say, which isn't exactly the truth.

"Well, I think it's great Edie wants you to stay there. It'll be like having your own place."

"Exactly. For a while anyway. As long as I stay." I glance around the room again, kicking at a few dead leaves. "What is this place?"

"Not much of anything."

"But it could be." I visualize Coffee for the Sole next door. "Why can't you enlarge the shop? You could tear down the wall and double the size."

"It's a load-bearing wall," Silas explains. "We need it there."

"Then what about a door? Or maybe..." I suck in my breath and look wildly at Silas. "Why don't you open something new?"

"I've thought of that a few times, but I'm—"

I don't let him finish because ideas are flying fast and furious. "When I was in town after the wedding, I went to The King's Hat with Sophie and we talked about how there needed to be a different kind of bar in town," I say, my words tumbling out. "One for women, with fancy cocktails and a dance floor."

I skate to the middle of the floor, and do a few dance moves. "Coffee and Cocktails," I decide. "You should open a bar. In here."

It's so clear in my mind: returning to Laandia and coming here for a drink with Sophie and Edie and Leodie. Dancing and drinking too many pretty cocktails. All my favourite bars and clubs rolled into one, but smaller.

The room could hold maybe twenty-five or thirty people. It would be perfect for girls' nights out or birthday parties—

"I don't have time to open anything other than the coffee shop in the morning." Silas sounds tired as he runs his hand through his hair, making the top stand up for a brief moment before slumping over. I think that means he needs a haircut, but now isn't the time to tell him that. "I don't have much disposable income to open something new," he admits.

"Then let me do it within your budget."

Budget. I don't think I've ever said that world out loud before.

I'm the daughter of a billionaire. I've never had a money problem in my life. If I want to buy something, I buy it. I treat my friends to dinner, to trips to our vacation homes, my father's yacht. I don't understand when people question prices or affordability, budgets or overspending.

But I do hear the worry in Silas's voice.

"I can pay for it."

His mouth falls open and he blinks at me with surprise. "No," he says quickly.

"But I can. I want to."

"No."

"Silas, you're my friend..."

"Stop saying that," he snaps. "There is absolutely no way or reason that I would let you pay for the construction of my business. Not unless you buy the building from me, and why would you do that if you're leaving soon? I wouldn't let you."

He sounds angry at the fact.

"But..." I could buy the building. Then I wouldn't have to go through Silas's worry to do this.

"No. Fenella, no. You can't buy everything."

"But I can," I whisper. "Okay, sorry," I add as he gives me a furious stare. "You don't have to open a bar or any new business... yet. But how about letting me use the space?"

"What do you want to use it for?"

I think quickly. "A party. A birthday party—for me."

SILAS

I'VE NEVER HEARD FENELLA speak so quickly. And with so much excitement.

Fenella doesn't show much emotion, other than the odd bit of disdain but suddenly, she's bouncing like a teenage girl at a Taylor Swift concert.

She thinks I should open a bar?

It's overwhelming how ideas and plans are pouring out, some fully formed, some sounding—pink cocktails made with local products? Bachelorette and birthday parties? Underage nights?

A Battle of the Bands?

But then—a birthday party?

"When is your birthday?" With all the time I've spent with Fenella in the last few days, it seems impossible that I don't know this fact.

"Two days before Halloween. We can—"

"That's in a week. You want to plan a party in a week?"

"I've done it before."

"But you had people to help you."

"You won't help?" The surprise in her voice cuts through me. "I can do it myself," she adds quickly, her voice chilling. "I would like to rent the place to have a party here."

The place has been empty for years. My parents bought the building as an investment property. It used to be pizza place but closed when the owner passed away. They thought someone would open a bakery or a café because of the tiny kitchen, and they would rent out the apartment upstairs.

It worked out just as they planned, except it was a sleazy insurance broker who wanted it and ended up scamming the people of Battle Harbour by getting them to invest in plans that would protect them from storms.

And when the first storm hit, he vanished, along with all of their money.

Since then, I haven't had the heart to make much of a push to find someone else. And Dad hated the idea of selling it because he's always full of ideas, just like Fenella.

Once or twice over the years, I've had the idea of an after-school learning centre where kids could get tutored or learn about science. But I hadn't done anything about it. The shop and Wyatt take up most of my time, and what I do have left, I give to the stars and my dreams about starting an observatory. I don't have the energy for something new.

But Fenella seems to. She seems to have a lot of energy for this.

She starts pointing things out; a bar would go *there*, a couch and chairs would be good *there* by the window, and would a dance floor be perfect *there*? A good paint job would do wonders, and the right lighting, plus a cocktail menu that would rock my world.

"It'll be a new place. And it'll be fantastic." Her words bubble out like a pot boiling over.

I finally manage to get a word in edgewise. "You want to have a party here?"

"Yes, Silas, that's what I've been saying," Fenella says patiently. "And if it's a success—which of course it will be—I think you should think about opening it as a bar."

"I don't know. I mean we don't really need another bar in town." Fenella stares at me. "Do we?"

"A place where a woman can get dressed up, have a decent martini, and dance until her feet hurt? Yes, you do."

She sounds very convinced. And convincing.

"I don't even live here, but I know what you need. Or at least I know what the female population needs. I've visited every drinking establishment around here, and The King's Hat is the only one where I felt remotely safe to show up on my own. But there's nowhere to dance." Fenella spins around and does a little shimmy that I watch with entirely too much interest. "It would be perfect. Small, exclusive... you could rent it out for parties, like mine. No sports paraphernalia, no obnoxiously drunk fishermen groping and grabbing—"

"You've been groped here?"

Fenella rolls her eyes. "This would be the perfect place for a group of girls to go for a night out—"

"Without men?"

Fenella shakes off the idea. "Men could come but they're not needed. Doesn't that sound like a great idea?"

A place where men aren't needed? Not really, no. "Would you invite men to your party?"

"Are you asking if I'd invite *you*?" She smiles. "Of course. I created a speakeasy in our basement for my brother's surprise twenty-first birthday. I got permits and bought alcohol and created the drinks and ordered food and the keg and..." She lifts her hands. "And I got a great DJ."

"Okay, but..." I shrug helplessly, not wanting to burst her bubble.

"I'll clean it up myself and paint it," Fenella continues. "Pink. I think that would be perfect."

"Have you ever painted anything?" I ask.

Fenella lifts her chin. "I've painted ceramics. And many toenails. I can ask Sophie to help. She's an artist. It's not that big of a space. We can do it in a night."

I turn in a circle, studying the space and trying to see it like Fenella does. She's planned it out in her head, and I can only see dirt and dust and the pile of leaves that has blown in through the open window. But still... "Okay," I say, like there was any doubt I'd agree.

"I can have a party?" Fenella gasps. "Oh, Silas, it'll be so much fun!"

I see her coming as if it's in slow motion—Fenella, dark hair flying, tiny sweater pulling up to show smooth skin and a sweet belly button marred by a diamond ring, throws her arms around my neck and presses into me.

She's hugging me. This is *not* the way to keep my distance. "You're the best, Silas!"

Oh, Lord, she smells so good. Like cherries. Dark cherries that have been warmed on a barbeque, if that makes sense.

She smells delicious.

And she feels even better.

"You really think you can do this in a week?" I ask, my arms tightening around her. It's just a hug—I don't need to hold her like this, but I can't let go.

Don't want to. It's been a while since I've held a woman like this.

And Fenella seems content like this, lying her head on my shoulder and breathing into my neck. Leaning against me, she's taller than I thought. I would only need to lean down a bit to— "I know I can do it," she says. "When is the meteor shower? The Draconids one?"

Being so close makes my head spin. "What? But—you remembered the name?"

"It sounds like dragons, so of course."

Of course. "It's... it's just after Halloween. Why?"

Fenella's arms squeeze my waist and then she pulls back with purple eyes sparkling. "I have another idea."

"That sounds ominous." The way this conversation has jumped around, I wouldn't be surprised if she wanted to go out and collect a meteor and somehow use it for her bar.

And I would be just fine with that. I would probably help her.

"It's not ominous. I have good ideas."

"You want to open a bar. Forgive me if I'm a little afraid of your ideas."

"You'll like this one." Her hands are still at my waist and she glances up under her lashes and for a moment I think—

"What did you want to show me?" I detangle from her grip reluctantly.

"Oh, I forgot." Fenella steps back and picks up the bag she dropped during one of her dances. "This."

She pulls out a cream-coloured woollen toque, with an enormous pink pom-pom. "So I can stay warm when you show me the stars again," she laughs.

Fenella

I'M STILL EXCITED WHEN I get back to the castle, my mind a whirl of ideas about the party. It will be my last night staying at the castle, so I feel like I should stay for dinner, even though I want nothing more than to throw my things in the car and move into Edie's.

And then make plans for my party.

Dining with the royal family of Laandia is like having a meal at a local diner but cooked by a world-renowned chef. It takes a little to get used to when you consider the setting—a castle.

This may be the small dining room, but the table can still hold from twelve to twenty guests. The settings may be simple, but it's Wedgewood and I can check my lipstick in the shine of the spoons. And I have been present when Gunnar and Princess Lyra performed a musical medley with the crystal wine glasses.

It's very different from dinners with my parents.

When it's just the family, no one dresses for dinner. There's a variety of denim in the dining room when I appear, and a few flannel shirts. I shouldn't be surprised, since the last time I was here, the meal was chicken tenders—succulent chunks of chicken breast, breaded with panko and Parmesan and more herbs and spices than KFC, but chicken strips, nonetheless.

King Magnus likes the simple things in life.

There are only two princes in attendance today—Kalle, the eldest, and Gunnar, the youngest. But the princesses-to-be are here: Stella is with Gunnar, and Edie with Kalle. This leaves Spencer Laz as the eligible bachelor for me to practice my smiles on.

Tempting, but not my type. I'm not sure what Spencer does for the family—he's a lawyer and the son of Duncan Laz, who is basically the right-hand man of the king—and he's known as the unofficial fifth prince of Laandia. But it's not his status that has me hesitating.

Unofficially, there's always been something going on between him and Princess Lyra. No one in the family will admit or acknowledge it, or even allow the thought to be spoken, but it's there. Call it a woman's intuition.

And if the only daughter of the king of Laandia has staked her claim on Spencer, then I will not be stepping foot on her territory. There are many women that I would go up against, but Princess Lyra is not one of them.

Prince Gunnar has a glass of wine for me as soon as I walk into the dining room. "Fen! Did I hear right? You're working at Coffee for the Sole?"

I lift a shoulder. "You're deserting me, so I need something to do. I like the way Silas makes my lattes, so why not hang out there?"

"Is that the only thing you like about Silas?" Stella demands in her no-nonsense way.

I glance at Edie before I answer. My thoughts about my new boss are a little confusing—okay, a lot confusing—but I don't need to share that with this group, especially if Edie will be delivering another lecture about how I should steer clear of her cousin. "He's a sweetheart," I say instead.

Before I can say anything else, King Magnus enters like a late summer windstorm. I've never met a person with a more charismatic presence than the king, and I've known my fair share of royals and celebrities and Very Important People. It's as if Tom Cruise, Oprah Winfrey, Lionel Messi and Keanu Reeves were shaken and stirred together—that would give you King Magnus.

The king, followed by Duncan, makes his apologies and greets his children before turning to me. "Ah, Fenella. I heard you roaring in from town in that yellow firecracker. So glad you took it off Coy's hands—that car was wasting away on his front lawn." He accepts the glass of wine Gunnar hands him and grins down at me.

"Your Majesty." I drop into a perfect curtsey. "It's a fun car. I should take you for a ride in it."

"I will take you up on that," he says, aiming for the head of the table. "I don't know why I've never got myself a muscle car. Seems like fun."

The king takes his seat, the sign for the rest of us to sit. "What happens to the car when you go home?" Stella asks.

"I haven't figured that out yet." I take the seat across from her, beside Edie. "I'll donate it to a worthy Laandian probably. Maybe Wyatt, if he gets his license."

"And you're working for Silas," Duncan says. He's like the king's shadow, if shadows were sixty-plus and still as handsome as a model on the cover of a romance novel, which is what Duncan used to do. "He makes darn good coffee."

"I also make darn good coffee," I tell him. "It's the only reason I persuaded him to hire me."

"We've had a few requests from reporters to enter the country," the king tells me. "You're still interesting."

"That will never change," Gunnar says fondly.

"I appreciate you keeping them away from me," I tell Magnus. "I'm not sure how you're doing it, but it's very nice."

"Don't want your first day of work splashed across the tabloids?" the king guffaws.

I shudder. "Definitely not."

What would people think of me working for Silas? A Billionaire Brat getting her hands dirty making coffee for the masses? They'd think it was a lark, a prank, that somehow, I was doing this only to make a grand announcement about some coffee-based skin moisturizer.

Not one of my millions of followers would believe that I'm working at Coffee for the Sole because I want to. That I *like* it. It's been fun making coffee and talking to the customers and getting to know Leodie and Jem.

And Silas.

For once, I don't care what other people think.

"I had an idea for that store beside the coffee shop," I tell Edie and Stella. "The one that's sitting empty."

"They made the best pizza back in the day," Edie reminisces.

"I thought Silas could open a club, targeting younger women who want a place to go. To dance, serve fun cocktails instead of beer. Although your honey mead is very tasty," I add to the king.

"Another bar in town?" Gunnar asks. "We'll be seeing more of Lyra coming home in that case."

"A dance club?" Stella frowns. "Like with the bright flashing lights and the *boom chicka boom* music?"

Gunnar and Kalle share a glance. "I'm not sure that kind of music," I offer. "But maybe a little stage area? You could sing." Stella inherited her father's musical ability.

"Maybe," she hedges.

"I think it's a great idea," Edie says, her dark eyes lit with excitement. "I would love to go someplace for a drink without someone asking me for a beer."

"I think you're talking about competition, and I *don't* think it's a good idea," Kalle grumbles.

"This will target a very different customer," Edie reminds him. "The King's Hat isn't really a girlie bar."

"Call it the Queen's Hat," Stella suggests with a mischievous grin.

"No," Kalle rumbles.

"Women looking for a good time. Sign me up," Gunnar says. Stella's grin fades and she gives him a sharp look. "I mean... you would have a wonderful time there," he adds to Stella.

"And as a trial run, I'm having my birthday party there," I tell them, thinking I should throw Gunnar a rescue.

Gunnar groans. "Not another Fenella birthday party. I don't think Battle Harbour has recovered from the last one."

Five years ago, Gunnar brought our friends for a visit to celebrate my birthday. It had been a great few days, but I feel this year might be a little different. I'm older, wiser.

My friends will be here, but so will Silas.

It's surprising how much I want him to be there.

"I remember that night," Kalle says in his gruff voice. "You're not stepping foot in my bar with that birthday ribbon thing again." But he says it with a grin.

"Which is why I'm making my own bar," I tell him with a cheeky smile.

And then I feel the king's gaze on me. "You think we need another drinking hole? Guess you best tell me more," he invites. "Because anything that makes my people happy is good for business."

Instead of telling him of my plans, I switch the subject. "Did you know Silas would like to build an observatory like in Nova Scotia?" I ask him instead. "He'd love to showcase Laandia as a destination for star-gazing. People go to Iceland and the Northern Territories to see the northern lights but there are just as good spots in Laandia."

King Magnus glances at Duncan and then Kalle. "I have to say, I never considered what's in the sky above us," he admits.

"I think it would be an excellent boost for tourism. He's taken me out to see the stars twice, and I have to say, the views are very impressive."

I try to ignore how Edie's head jerks toward me when I mention Silas taking me out.

"I know a lot of people who would pay a lot of money to be able to see the northern lights here," I continue. "Not to mention the stars."

King Magnus looks over at Duncan. "Could be something to think about. When you get your club set up, why don't you and Silas come and talk to us?"

Silas will be so excited—if he forgives me for bringing this to the king. I have a feeling he will.

I'm impossible to stay angry with.

"That would be great," I say. "He'll be so happy."

"Happy people are good for business," he repeats, giving me a wide smile, the one that would make even the hardest heart melt.

SILAS

WHEN I CLOSE UP, I wait until Leodie and Jem are out of sight, and then I go next door.

Now that Fenella has gone back to the castle, I can think clearly about this. No man could think straight with her so happy, smiling and laughing. Dancing.

Hugging me.

I may have decided to keep my distance, but Fenella didn't help by throwing her arms around me. Twice.

The first time she hugged me, I was so overwhelmed to have her suddenly in my arms that I forgot to put the brakes on her ideas until I can sort things out.

The second time, I may have forgotten my name.

But now with only the ghost of Fenella dancing in the empty space, I can look at it like she did.

That's not easy for me.

Mia was always able to see the potential. It was she who could view a life for us outside Battle Harbour. She had ideas, plans—it would have been a good life, I realized too late. But it wasn't the life I wanted. That was here. With my family and my friends and Coffee for the Sole to run. I couldn't even think about living anywhere else. Back then, I missed home even before I went anywhere.

Now? I don't know. I know I never gave Mia the respect of *really* listening to what she wanted, so caught up in my unease of the possibility of leaving that I ignored what *she* needed.

I feel bad about that. But I don't feel the familiar hurt and regret when I think of her, and that's a good thing.

I look her up every once in a while, which is why I don't do much on social media. If I log in, I search for pictures of Mia, of the life we could have had together. I don't regret not leaving—Fenella has a point of not regretting anything. And I'm not too fussed about not having anyone to share my life with—until I see someone I may want in my life.

I study the empty space and try to see it like Fenella does. Mia would be able to see it, and because of that, I let myself see it too.

The bar *here.* Tables *there*, on the side of the dance floor.

The floor is in good shape but it wouldn't hold up for long to a group of women dancing in high heels. I could look into a parquet overlay; a good-sized square.

"It could go *here.*" I wonder if that would get me a third hug.

Women dancing, laughing. The odd boyfriend, or a friend. This wouldn't be a place to meet men, just a spot for women to hang out. Dance. Laugh. Be together.

She wants to have her birthday party *here.*

Is this something that Fenella has in her life? A place like this that she wants to recreate here, in Battle Harbour?

I take out my phone to check on that theory.

A minute later, I've sunk into the rabbit hole of Fenella Carrington on social media, standing in what may become the newest hip and happening spot in Battle Harbour, if Fenella has her way.

It's easy to find her online: Google her name and a list of her most popular posts scrolls down the screen. Makeup tutorials, dance lessons, reels of her in the most beautiful clothes, with friends and escorts and famous people I recognize from movies and television and who call Fenella a friend.

There are tons of pictures of her with her group. They are celebrities in their own rights, but no one shines as much as Fenella does.

The Billionaire Brats.

I scroll through her posts. It's not difficult to notice the different expressions she has, each one giving me one more piece of the puzzle. There's the tight smile she used with Jonathan the other day—*I don't like you but I'm being polite*. The professional look—*I'm beautiful and I'm getting paid for it.*

My favourite smile is the one has when she's with her friends. Laughing. Eyes bright. Unconcerned.

I like it because that's the way she looks at me.

And then I give myself a mental kick—I'm supposed to be looking at the places she goes, not how she smiles. A few minutes later, I come to the conclusion this won't be a copy of anywhere. This is a new idea for Fenella.

If she gets caught up with it, maybe she'll stay longer. But that might be torture as well, because she'll still leave someday.

My sister Emily would have loved a place like this. She used to spend time with her girlfriends at the house, and I would watch them together and marvel at the mysteries of the female.

Maybe if there was a space for her, she might not have gotten messed up with Wyatt's father. Maybe she wouldn't have left.

That decides it for me. But I'm not about to tell Fenella just yet. She promised to create a business plan for a bar, and I think that would be a good thing.

I just don't know if it's going to be a good thing for me to work with her on this.

Can't be worse than working every day in the coffee shop.

Fenella

AFTER DINNER, I'M STILL high on my ideas, so I suggest we head into town so I can check out the competition.

"A reconnaissance mission," I say to Gunnar, knowing he loves the idea of anything adventurous.

He almost doesn't agree because Stella isn't keen on the idea—it's too late, they're leaving the next day, she's tired. It's Edie who convinces her. She and Kalle both have the night off and are game to continue the family fun.

"But we're not going to my place," Kalle says. "You've been there enough. You know what it's like."

Spencer comes with us, and Duncan and King Magnus agree to one drink at a bar.

Barhopping with the royal family.

Not an unusual night for me.

"No pictures," Gunnar warns me as we tumble out of the two SUVs. The security team brought us into town, parking in front of our first stop, Geri and Freki's.

"Want to take my phone to make sure?" I offer it to him.

"I trust you."

I push it at him. "Seriously, take it. I can't stop taking the worst pictures when I'm drinking."

He gives a chortle of laughter and pockets my phone. "Remember that night on Milo's father's yacht? I think it was in Greece somewhere and you and Lavinia were doing shots. You took that horrible picture when she was about to throw up—"

"And she *did* throw up, all over the phone—"

"Only it was Rupert's phone," Gunnar finishes, slapping his thigh at the memory.

I laugh with him until I catch sight of Stella, standing behind Gunnar. She doesn't look angry or jealous but somewhat uneasy. Out of place.

Pulling Stella over, I tuck my arm in hers and lead her into the bar. "Do you do shots?" I ask conversationally.

"I've been known to," she says carefully.

"Well, that's something we have in common, because so do I. Hello," I say to the bartender, who greets us with a frown, that quickly changes to shock and awe when he notices King Magnus behind me.

"Your Majesty—" he breathes, looking old enough to have been around for the previous king.

I wiggle my finger in his face. "You're talking to me first, so focus. I need shots for all—a round of Jäegarbombs." I stand on my tiptoes to see over the bartender's shoulder. "Maybe not, because I'm not seeing it there. Irish whiskey?"

"We're not drinking Irish whiskey," Magnus roars. "We'll drink my mead."

"Shots first," Gunnar tells him, crowding beside Stella.

"Fireballs?" I suggest. "Do you mind if I come back there to take care of this?" I ask the bartender. I think we might have overwhelmed him, because he can only nod, eyes full of amazement darting from one royal to another.

"Don't you ever come in here?" I ask Gunnar as I slide around to the other side of the bar.

"We go to Kalle's. He gets pouty if we don't."

"Is this okay, Wade?" Kalle asks the bartender.

"Sure, fine, be my guest," he mutters.

"Hello, Wade, I'm Fenella." I smile brightly as he stands with a stunned expression off to the side. "Give me a minute and I'll show you how to make a tasty treat, even if His Majesty has something about the Irish. And while I'm doing that, can you tell me who Geri and Freki are, and if they're here tonight? Since your fine establishment is named after them, I think it would be nice if we met."

I pour a round of Irish Car Bombs for everyone, and then a pitcher of honey mead. I discover that Geri and Freki, are not people, but the original King Odin's—he of Asgard, not Laandia—pet wolves.

This leads to a discussion as we continue on to the next bar—which is called Midgard—if Silas's club should have a Viking name.

At Midgard, Kalle and Stella—who warmed up after the Irish whiskey shot and went head-to-head with Gunnar in chugging a beer—push me behind the bar again. Since this is more of an upbeat place that caters to the younger crowd, they have a better-stocked liquor supply and I make candy corn shots to celebrate Halloween early.

"What do you think Silas should call it?" I ask Stella after we come back from the dance floor. It was a small, uneven space, and it was just the two of us dancing to Taylor Swift's country era, but I felt it was important to experience everything the bar had to offer.

"Why don't you ask him?" She grins.

I cock my head. "Do you know, I don't even have his number? This place is so small that it's no trouble to track him down. Gunnar has my phone," I add. "I need to make sure I get that back before you leave."

"You don't need Silas's number to talk to him." Stella puts a hand on my shoulder to stop me, then turns me toward the doorway.

Silas is walking into the bar.

Right now. Into Midgard, where I have drunk half a pink to the king's delicious honey mead and two candy corn shots and am now trying to dance everything out of my system.

He's here.

"He's here?" I gasp, clapping my hands. "Is he real or did that candy corn shot make things wonky?"

"I called Sophie, so they're both here, but yeah—I do feel a little wonky." But Stella still drags me over to where Silas and Sophie are greeting the king.

"Congratulations on hiring this force of nature," Magnus is telling Silas as I desert Stella and skip over to them.

"Hi," I say, unable to tone down the smile on my face. Silas has changed his shirt from the one he was wearing earlier today to a long-sleeved gray shirt that hugs parts of him that I would love to hug. "Hi."

"Hi." Silas turns away from the king of Laandia to smile down at me—which would be tantamount to treason in some countries but makes me feel really good.

"Hi," I repeat, my smile only getting wider.

"What's with all the 'hi's," Kalle grumbles, but he crowds Silas out to speak to his father.

Which leaves Silas to talk to me.

"This is fun," he says, leaning down so I can hear him over the music. "Family time with the king?" I haven't drunk enough to miss the flash of uncertainty cross his face, so I hand him my half-empty pint of honey mead.

"It is fun! I told them at dinner all about the idea for a bar and when I said I needed a renaissance—reco-sauce... a fact-finding mission," I manage— "they all decided to come with. FYI—" I lean against Silas's arm, which suddenly slips behind my back in a very smooth move. "Sir Duncan is *very* attractive."

"Yes, he is," Silas agrees with a chuckle. He rests his hand gently on my hip, and alcohol or not, I like the feel of it there.

"So are you," I decide. "Why don't you like pumpkin spice?"

"I—what?"

"You don't like pumpkin spice," I point out. "But it's strange because—" I lean closer, almost resting my head on the wide breadth of his chest. "You kind of smell like it."

"Are you smelling me?" he asks in a low voice, with the kind of tone that curls around your insides.

"I—kind of, yes. You smell good," I confess.

"You smell really good, too. Like cherries." He looks as surprised as I am that those words just came out of his mouth. "And right now, a variety of alcohol."

"I'm not surprised," I say with a laugh. "You need to smell like that too. C'mon. Time to catch up. Next stop?" I call to the others.

"Sailor's Salon?" Gunnar asks.

"What about Ragnarok?" Edie demands.

"Oooh, let's go there," I cheer. "That was fun last time."

King Magnus lifts his empty glass, looking so much like a Viking—albeit one in a faded concert T-shirt and ratty jeans—that I wish I kept my phone to take a picture. "To Ragnarok!" he cries.

SILAS

I LIVE IN A country with a monarchy. We are ruled by a king who is just and kind and benevolent to his people.

I had no clue King Magnus could slam back a shot like that.

I'm seeing a new side of the royal family, which leaves me feeling like I've stepped through the wardrobe into Narnia. I've never seen Prince Kalle look so happy, keeping a hand on Edie at all times and looking down at her with such devotion in his eyes that it's like he's a different person from the gruff former athlete who still shows up to throw balls with the high school team.

King Magnus looks like Gunnar when he grins, and he does that constantly, keeping up at least three different conversations at once and bringing anyone within arm's reach into his orbit.

He is the sun here in Battle Harbour tonight and the rest of us rotate around him, hoping for a bit of his warmth.

I understand now why men will go to battle for their king.

After three shots—shaken and stirred by Fenella behind the bar—and a pint of honey mead, I realize there is no way I can catch up to the others.

But it's still fun to try.

Ragnarok is where the LGBTQ community hangs out, so the dance floor is wide and packed, the music a loud and cheerful mix of 1990s boy band pop and recent hits. After Fenella's bartender stint is over, I pull her out onto the dance floor.

"You like to dance?" she asks with amazement, raising her voice so I can hear her over NSYNC.

"Love it." I move my shoulders, wiggle my hips, and Fenella claps her hands with delight.

"I love that you love it, because I love to dance." She does a few of the Bye, Bye Bye moves, and a space opens for us on the dance floor.

I wave to a few people that I recognize, but all the attention is on Fenella. Apparently, she has a huge following within the LGBTQ community here in Battle Harbour. There is shrieking, a few screams, a lot of hugging and countless selfies taken with her.

She smiles and accepts the adoration, but her gaze keeps returning to me.

I keep smiling and nodding and do my best to keep her in sight.

This is so much better than watching her social media posts. Fenella tonight seems like a different person from last night. It could be the alcohol, but I think it's something else.

Last night, we sat on a bench and looked at the stars. Now, she's showing off her moves to an entire bar full of admiring fans. She's getting as much or more attention than the king.

That could be because the vest she's wearing sparkles like a disco ball. It's covered in sequins—

No, they're crystals. Her vest—worn with no shirt underneath—is covered entirely in crystals.

It shines as much as she does. Her confidence is awe-inspiring. How many people can go bar-hopping with the royal family and not turn into a simpering sycophant?

Look at me—King Magnus is beside me, dancing to ABBA and I have to fight the urge to drop into a bow like a proper courtier. I've lived my whole life in Battle Harbour, and I've spoken to him once.

Now I'm dancing right beside him.

When the DJ notices the king and Duncan Laz out on the floor, ABBA changes into "Want You," which was Kräftig's biggest hit.

King Magnus and Duncan Laz used to be in a heavy metal band. The monarchy of Laandia has always been a little bit different.

This is what Fenella's life is like all of the time.

We stay for another few songs and then head out to Sailor's Salon, where the few patrons holding up the bar don't blink at the sight of their king's sudden appearance.

He buys a round for everyone there.

Fenella nudges me with her shoulder. "Having fun?" The lights are dimmer and her vest doesn't sparkle as much as it did in Ragnarok.

But she still sparkles. She shines, and it's hard for me to take my eyes off her.

"I was head-banging with the king. That's not my usual evening entertainment."

She grins, eyes sparkling as much as her vest. "You'll always have fun with me."

"I've never doubted that."

"Then why don't you want to kiss me?"

She catches me with my pint glass halfway to my mouth. I pause and then take a much-needed mouthful of local IPA. "I never said I didn't want to kiss you," I say carefully after I swallow.

"You didn't say it, but it seems like that." She looks down, smile fading.

"I don't think we should talk about this right now," I suggest, at a loss for what to do. She seems... disappointed? That I don't want to kiss her?

"We probably won't talk about it at all because I'm horrible at expressing my emotions. I over-react." She enunciates carefully. "That's what my parents say."

I really dislike her parents. "I think you're doing a great job expressing your emotions."

"The alcohol helps." Fenella's expression clears like the sky after a quick summer rain. "We had a lot of wine with dinner."

"While you were dining with the royal family."

"I was." She squints at me—possibly trying to read what I'm not saying, or maybe because she's had too much to drink. "Does that bother you?"

"Nothing that you do could bother me, Fenella."

"Because we're friends."

She thinks we're friends. And we are.

While it's fun to be friends with Fenella, I can't help where my mind goes at night. Or during the day—watching her smile at the customers, making them feel like they're the most important people in her world right then.

I like her. More than I should. She's not going to be here forever, so there's no point wishing on whatever falling star that brought Fenella to me. I've already had my heart broken once and don't need to go through that again.

"I think my ride is leaving," Fenella says in a glum voice.

I glance over her shoulder. The group is gathering coats, finishing drinks. Gunnar looks over at Fenella and gestures to the door. "I thought you were staying at Edie's."

"Tomorrow. I don't have my things." Fenella leans toward me. "I guess I better go."

"Or you'll turn into a pumpkin?"

She touches my arm, runs her hand along my bicep. "I don't think I've ever seen you not wearing flannel. I miss it." I swallow as she drifts even closer, her cheek brushing against my shoulder. "I'll miss you," she whispers.

My heart gives a leap like it's doing an Olympic-worthy high dive.

She's been drinking. That much is clear. But that's not why she's saying these things. There is something here between us. I felt it from the start, only I never expected Fenella to feel it too. But still...

My hand moves of its own accord, pushing back strands of hair that cling to her cheek. It's soft, silky to the touch.

"Fenella," I begin.

"Silas." There's a challenge in her purple eyes; those eyes that hold me captive and have since the first time I saw her.

Out of the corner of my eye, I see Gunnar and Stella move toward the door with the others. Fenella is leaving with the family. Is leaving...

It would be so easy to touch her lips with mine. Take her in my arms and kiss her with every ounce of my want.

But still... "I don't know..." It breaks the spell, pops the bubble around us, and transforms Fenella's hopeful expression. "I don't know if you... I don't know."

Disappointment floods her face. "I don't know either," she confesses. "Can we just not know? See what happens?"

"But you're leaving." The lump in my throat makes it difficult to swallow.

"Yes," she murmurs. She swallows and her lips part. All it would take is for me to lean down and brush my lips against hers.

I want to. I want to kiss her so much—I want the others to leave and keep her here with me and...

She touches my chest.

Fenella lifts a hand and rests it on my chest, curling her fingers slightly like she's fisting my shirt in her hand and for one horrified moment, I think she's going to kiss me.

And then she pats my chest and steps back. I draw in a ragged breath. "Good night, Silas," she says with resignation.

"Good night, Fenella."

I walk her outside, and she doesn't look back as she takes her spot in the royal caravan back to the castle.

It's for the best that nothing happened.

Because if Fenella Carrington kisses me, there is no way I'll ever be able to let her go.

I stand on the sidewalk with Sophie as we wave goodbye. The hour is late and the moon swings high in the sky. Clouds scud along, obscuring many of the stars. I can make out Polaris at the tip of Ursa Minor.

"That was fun," Sophie bubbles. "And totally unexpected."

"Uh-huh." I stare at the SUV until it turns the corner.

"You seem a bit stunned," she says, tucking an arm around my waist.

"I was head-banging with the king," I tell her numbly.

"Yes, but are you stunned because of King Magnus or Fenella?" Sophie asks.

I don't feel the need to answer that.

Fenella

Me: We need to make honey mead a global sensation

Lavinia: that sounds medieval

Ashton: isn't that what they drink in Laandia

Milo: did you go out without us? Bad girl

Me: You'll see me soon! Party for my birthday! Here

Rupert: Here as in…??

Me: Laandia. Battle Harbour

Lavinia: In the castle!

She sends a variety of emojis of castles and crowns and excited faces.

> Me: Even better

> Milo: What's better than a castle and all those princes?

My club, I decide.

> Coral: Send deets and I'll get them there.

Coral will make sure everyone is there, and while of course I want my friends around to celebrate my birthday, I have to wonder what Silas will think of them.

And what they will think of Silas.

I think a lot about Silas—more than I should for someone who may not be thinking of me.

I like Silas. I like him as a person, and I like him more than a friend. I'm fairly certain he feels the same way.

If this were the old Fenella, even three-week-ago Fenella, I would take Silas's lack of action in pursuing me and make him fall for me. I could do it to. I've done it before—make a man fall in love with me when he really didn't want to.

I'm very fall-in-lovable. But long-term-lovable?

I haven't managed to become that for anyone.

But do I want to be that for Silas? It's clear he does not want anything more than what we have—spending time together at the shop. Spending time together outside work. Looking at the stars on dark nights, which has to be one of the most romantic things I've ever done with anyone, and I'm doing it with a man who only wants to be my friend.

Has Silas *friend-zoned* me? Because I'm not staying in Battle Harbour for the unforeseeable future? There's nothing I can do about that... except to stay.

I wouldn't even follow my fiancé around the country while he was on tour. There's no way I'm about to relocate for someone.

Not yet.

But what if...

A text chimes from an unknown number.

> How are you feeling this morning?

> This is Silas btw

He texts me. Silas has texted me, and I didn't even know he had my number.

I can't stop the smile as my thumbs tap out a reply.

> Me: Great!!!

> Me: Actually... great. No exclamations point. I drank Screech again and I promised myself I wouldn't do that again.

> Silas: You really need to stay away from that stuff. I had a bad experience when I was younger and have managed to avoid it at all cost. Stick with the honey mead. Or the shots. You're a good bartender

> **Me:** Maybe I'll have to take a shot behind the bar at our club

It's getting easier to picture a life here. Just a sliver, like a crescent moon cresting over the waves. But I shut it down before it can grow because while Silas is a big part of why I'm enjoying my time in Laandia, I wouldn't stay just for him.

I'd have to stay for me.

> **Silas:** you should come in for coffee

Is that an invitation? An indication that he wants to see me?

He crashed the royal party last night. I think it's obvious he wants to see me.

Maybe he's just a slow mover. Likes the slow burn.

I'm not staying forever. I would really like to see how Silas can burn before it's time to go.

> **Me:** I might just do that. Who's working today?

> **Silas:** Leodie, me and Wyatt. I give him hours on the weekend when he doesn't have practice

> **Me:** Such a nice boss

> **Silas:** Because I let you sleep in?

I send a smiley face in return

Silas: back to work. See you soon?

Me: If you're lucky

Silas: I thought you were the lucky one

That gets me out of bed. Silas does want to see me. I never expected that Silas would become the one thing I can't wait to see in Laandia.

After breakfast, after I say goodbye to Gunnar and Stella, I pack my car with my things and drive into town to move in to Edie's.

It's a sunny day in Battle Harbour with a chill breeze tinged with salt blowing off the ocean. I park behind Edie's building and walk across the square.

Three people greet me by name, one person rushes up to me with an excited grin to talk about last night. He's someone I was dancing with at Ragnarok, but I haven't a clue what his name is.

It's obvious I made many friends last night.

The owner of the candy shop waves at me, and I stop to admire the container of fall flowers outside the flower shop. And then I go in to buy some.

Eventually, I make it to Coffee for the Sole. The doorbell chimes as I push the door open. The scent of coffee wafts to greet me, same as it always does, but the shop feels different today. Every table is full, with a lineup halfway to the door.

I'm greeted. Smiled at. Waved to.

Something happens inside me. Everything is warm, liquid, sweet, like a vat of honey that's been sitting in the sun.

"Fenella, I heard you were rocking out with the *king* last night." Mrs. Geordie stands before me with her flat white and an impressed smile. "I had a very memorable night dancing with him years ago, and I've never forgotten it."

"Duncan would be one I'd never forget a night with," Mrs. McKibbon chimes in. "That man keeps getting better with age."

"It was a fun night," I tell them, edging closer to the line. I look up to see Silas looking at me.

Smiling at me.

He holds up a pumpkin spice latte.

SILAS

I T'S AS IF I sensed her coming in.

I was making three pumpkin spice lattes for Gregor Maclean and his crew when I filled another cup and added a shot of vanilla. And then I looked up to see Fenella caught between Mrs. Geordie and Mrs. McKibbon.

The crystal vest is gone, but she still looks like she made an effort. Tight black pants and boots that come up to her knees with a purple sweater cropped at the waist and yet another jacket. This one is big and white and fluffy, and I'm sure it's fashionable, but it wouldn't look out of place in Stella's pet rescue centre.

The expression on her face when she catches sight of me holding the latte though is—

I don't think it's the beverage or the rescue that she's so happy to see.

"Hi," she says, finally wriggling her way to where I stand behind the coffee maker.

"Hi, yourself." I hand her the drink, holding her gaze with mine for as long as I can. "Move-in day?"

She nods. "The car is packed with my bags. A few more than I came with—" She gives a sheepish shrug.

"Who says Battle Harbour isn't a mecca for shopping?"

Fenella laughs. "You're busy today."

"It's because I'm working today," Wyatt cuts in, leaning across me. "It's always like this when I'm here."

"It's because it's the weekend," I correct with an elbow to his ribs.

Since last night, all I've been able to think about is how I wanted to kiss Fenella when I had the chance, and whether I did the right thing walking away. My first instinct is to protect my heart.

It's not easy and it's not fun but I came to the conclusion that it's the right thing to do.

Until Fenella walks in and I can't keep my eyes off her lips which are covered in a pearly pink gloss today.

"Is it true that Prince Kalle was *dancing* at Ragnarok last night?" Leodie demands from behind the cash register. "Silas won't give details."

"She means I won't show her pictures," I say.

"There's tons of pictures of you out there. Looks like you were having a great time," Leodie says.

"Wait until my party." Fenella winks. "I confirm he was dancing, but I didn't take any pictures to prove it either," she tells her with a shrug. "I gave Gunnar my phone because me with a camera after a couple of shots is never a good thing."

"Silas did *shots*." Leodie shakes her head. "What are you doing to him?"

Fenella catches my glance and it's like she holds it gently in her hands. "Showing him a good time, I hope."

"I had fun," I assure her. "I'm glad Stella texted me."

"Me too. I guess I could have, but I didn't have your number until about an hour ago." She grins.

"Bosses always have their employees' numbers," I say, not about to admit I asked Sophie for it last night.

"That's a good thing." She stands at the counter for a long moment, and we just look at each other.

"Silas, flat white," Leodie calls and breaks me from my stupor.

"I'll let you get back to work," she says.

"What are you up to today?" I ask, unwilling to let her walk out.

"Planning my party. Unpacking. Finding stuff to clean," she lists. "I'm coming over tomorrow morning with supplies. You won't even recognize next door when I'm done."

I stop myself from asking her if she's ever cleaned anything before. "Sounds good. I'll keep the lattes coming."

"I might need them. What do you have planned for a Saturday night in Battle Harbour?"

"Euchre night," I admit with a touch of embarrassment. "My parents have one once a month. It's a pretty big crowd."

"I had no idea you were a card sharp," she marvels. "I've never learned to play Euchre. Poker yes—anything else, I'm guaranteed to lose."

"Lots of trips to Las Vegas?"

"Strip poker with friends actually. I'm pretty good."

I have to bite my tongue not to comment on that.

Fenella gives a big wave and heads to the door. I watch her go, and then realize Leodie and Wyatt are watching me watch her.

"You like her," Leodie accuses once Fenella has left.

"You totally do," Wyatt agrees.

"Are you dating?" Despite the lineup, Leodie stands with hands on hips, staring at me. I'm not sure if she's offended by the thought of me dating Fenella or that I didn't tell her if I was.

Which I'm not. I'm not dating Fenella. A quick glance out the front window shows her halfway across the square, her white jacket as out of place here as a snowstorm in June.

"It's nothing," I assure her. "We're not dating."

"It would be great if you found someone," she says. "But she's *Fenella Carrington*."

"I know who she is."

"Do you really?" Leodie points Wyatt to the cash register before pulling out her phone. With a few scrolls of her fingers, there she is, Fenella talking to the camera as she rubs brown cream on her face with a brush. "Can you see the numbers on this, Si?"

"I don't know what I'm looking at."

"This is Fenella, using Nu-No contouring cream. She got over a million views."

"A million people watched her put cream on her face?"

"That's just one video. She has an entire series for Nu-No. They gave her a hundred thousand dollars to do it. And that's just one thing. Instagram is full of her."

"We're not dating," I tell her, not sounding very convincing, even to myself. Yes, I make a mental note to check out Instagram, but not here. I tap Leodie's phone. "That's great for her."

"She's Fenella Carrington. She's amazing and fun, and funny, and I think it's great she's working here, but she's still a beautiful gazillionaire who has people following her all over the world, not to mention the thousands who think they're in love with her." Leodie gives me a look and I know what she's not asking—am I one of the thousands who think they're in love with her?

It's as if Leodie is giving me a warning, or maybe a wake-up call. The only reason Fenella is here is because she's hiding out from the world. Once everyone forgets about her outburst, we'll never see her again. Or maybe when she's got another scandal splashed across the papers. She doesn't belong here, as much as I wish she did. "She's not a gazillionaire; her father is."

I chose not to comment on the beautiful part. Or the unspoken question of whether I'm in love with her.

Fenella

I DON'T REMEMBER THE last time I didn't have plans on a Saturday night or spent it alone without Coral or Ashton to hang out with.

I unpack my bags, hang clothes in Edie's closet, and prepare for some alone time tonight.

It's a surprise that the thought of it actually excites me.

I've always hated weekends when I didn't have plans. When my friends were busy, when I wasn't dating anyone, if Ashton was off doing his racing thing and I couldn't join him. I've always been an extrovert. A people person.

Coral was the only one who asked me if I was going to be okay going to Laandia on my own.

Now it doesn't seem so bad.

Once I hang things up, and am refreshed by the pumpkin spice flowing through my veins, I head back out to the hardware store to buy cleaning supplies.

The only thing I'll say about that trip is that Jim and Bob who work there had an enjoyable time teaching me the ins and outs of the various cleaning products.

Back at Edie's, I curl up on the couch with my laptop, Ernie the cat perched at my feet, watching me with suspicious yellow eyes as I get to work on party/opening bar planning.

I scour Pinterest and make a vision board. I work on a business plan. I've never actually made a spreadsheet, but thanks to a few YouTube videos, I do quite well with it.

Stella tells me about a Facebook group for small businesses in Battle Harbour, and I start calling around to get quotes on the work I think the place needs.

I really like the idea of creating a new bar for the town. I think it's exactly what the women of Battle Harbour need, and having my party there will show everyone.

While I'm doing this, I get to know Ernie the cat. He eventually lets me pet him and curls up at my side when I go to bed.

I talk to my father; via email, but it's still a conversation. He tells me things have begun to settle down. Only one person tagged me on Instagram last night, but it was a grainy picture and you couldn't really tell it was me.

I'm not sure how my father knows I'm no longer viral—possibly Peter, his assistant told him—but it's good news to me.

Plan on returning the coming weekend, he writes.

Next weekend? My birthday is Sunday night and that's when I planned the party for.

I'll stay an extra day, I've got plans for the weekend.

He counters with an email with an offer to show me around the company next Tuesday, maybe see about finding me a role that fits my skill level.

It's what I wanted, so where's the excitement? Why do I have this feeling of dread in the pit of my stomach?

I push it away. My life is not here. I'm not a part of this community, as much as they have welcomed me.

But part of me wants to be.

Sunday morning, I'm awake early, thanks to Ernie the cat. But it's a good thing.

It's cleaning day.

I have a week to get this place party ready.

Coffee for the Sole is not as busy when I push open the door, but then again, it's a lot earlier than yesterday. There are only a few customers at the tables absorbed in crossword puzzles and newspapers, and no one is in line as I prop my broom and mop against the wall with my bucket of supplies.

"Whatcha got there?" Wyatt calls to me. He's the only one behind the counter.

"I'm cleaning." I enunciate the word because it's a first for me. "Cleaning."

"So you said. Where are you cleaning?"

Silas comes out of the back room with a bottle of syrup in his hands. "Hey," he says with a surprised smile. "Hi."

"Hi." When I see Silas, it's like a light switch is turned on inside me, or a string of Christmas lights plugged in for the first time. I feel in focus, at attention.

I feel seen. Silas *sees* me.

I make my way to the counter on suddenly shaky legs. Silas makes me feel seen. Tiger...

Tiger only noticed himself with me. Lennon wanted me for arm candy. Emmanuel, Tamir, Stavros... no one made me feel like Silas does. Gunnar came close, but there's been no one—

"You okay?" Silas asks. He's back to wearing flannel—this one a simple blue, red, and white pattern that does nothing special to his eyes—and his scruffy beard is more scruff than beard. But he's smiling at me, the smile reaching his green eyes.

My stomach flutters like the leaves of a maple tree when an October wind blows through it.

"Great."

"No exclamation points on your great today?"

I shake my head. "Not this morning."

"Let's hope you get them back today. The regular, I assume?"

"Please. And a cinnamon bun. I think I need the sugar."

Wyatt stands firm behind the cash register, which means Silas, with a quick rueful shake of his head, makes my drink. "You just work weekends?" I ask Wyatt.

"And school holidays. Silas says I need to study more in my spare time, not fool around in here after school." Wyatt makes a face.

"You want to go to university, you need the grades," Silas tells him as he pumps syrup into my cup.

"He's right," I say.

"Where did you go to school?" Wyatt asks me.

"I did a semester at UCLA, but school was never my thing. I started modeling then and you can't be in Europe and a classroom at the same time." That semester I spent in college feels so long ago.

It was also the last time I felt like a regular person, at least before I came here.

"I wish I finished though," I add. "I really think I missed out on a lot. Where do you want to go?"

"Montreal." Wyatt sounds excited just saying the name, but by the expression on Silas's face, he clearly doesn't share the excitement.

"Montreal is a great place."

"I have one more year of high school, and then I'm gone."

"You've got it all planned out."

"I can't wait." Wyatt sounds impossibly young. Or maybe it's just in the light, he looks less like a clone of Silas. As he warms up my cinnamon bun, Wyatt chatters about his plans for the future.

None of which seem to involve staying in Laandia.

My heart hurts for Silas, who listens to Wyatt without saying a word. Another person he loves will leave him.

I don't want to hurt him.

SILAS

I CAN HEAR FENELLA next door.

She has Taylor Swift turned up loud enough for me to hear it faintly, as well as the odd snippet of Fenella occasionally singing. There's some thumping, one crash that almost had me running over to check on her.

I really doubt she's ever cleaned anything in her life.

The temptation of going in to see how it's going is strong, but I resist until lunchtime. And then I tell Leodie I have an errand and run out to the bakery to get two sandwiches.

Even though I live next door, I always bring my lunch, because it's never a quick trip if I run next door. I'll finish the dishes, throw on a load of laundry, or check something on my PC.

Today I don't feel like the leftover stew I brought from home.

I knock on the door, bakery bag in my hand, and then ease it open. "Feel like taking a break?" I call.

Fenella backs out of one of the bathrooms, rubber gloves up to her elbows and a facemask over her mouth and nose. "Hi," she says, voice muffled. "A break sounds good."

She peels off the gloves and leaves them on the floor along with the mask. She's braided her dark hair into two plaits and then tied them in little buns at the back of her head, which makes her look much younger. I pull the table out from the kitchen, wincing at the uneven legs. "I feel horrible that this is such a mess and you have to clean it up," I burst out.

"Don't be." She follows me with two chairs. "It's fun."

"Really?"

"Well, maybe not cleaning the bathrooms. I don't know if you believe this, but I've never cleaned anything in my life."

"I believe it." I hand her a turkey on rye, with avocado and spinach. I guessed what she'd like.

Fenella looks around with consternation. "It doesn't look bad, does it?"

"It looks great," I assure her. "Almost like a new place. I just thought that with your lifestyle, housekeeping wouldn't be something you usually do."

"Ah. No." She shakes her head. "First time cleaning a toilet."

"You'll remember it forever," I tease. "We could go upstairs to my place," I add. "If this isn't..."

"This is fine. Thank you for bringing me lunch. It was really sweet of you."

"I didn't think you'd stop," I admit, handing her a bottle of water. "I've heard you banging all morning. It sounds like you haven't taken a break."

"I've done a lot." There's pride in her tone as she looks around, taking in the ceiling corners without the cobwebs, the piles of dust and dirt and leaves swept up and inside a black garbage bag. "I'm going to wash everything once I finish the bathroom."

"For someone's first time, you're pretty speedy." I take a bite of my roast beef sandwich.

"You'd be surprised what a YouTube video can teach you."

I laugh, and Fenella grins at my reaction. "It was nice to see Wyatt there today."

"He's there most weekends. It gives him some spending money, plus I think it's good for kids to have a job. I mean," I stammer, forgetting that before I hired her, Fenella had never had a regular job.

"I agree. My first "job"—" she uses her fingers as quotation marks— "—was for the family company. When I was ten, my father let Ashton and me pick the colours for the new toy cars. He left us with Evan—"

"Who's Evan?" I ask, hungrier to know more about Fenella than I am for lunch.

Fenella looks surprised. "My older brother."

"You have another brother?"

"Unfortunately." She laughs. "He's ten years older than us and I've never been his favourite sister."

"But you're his only sister?"

"Exactly. Evan tolerates Ashton because the racing brings in money for the company, and Evan is nothing if not a company man. He'll run the whole place when Dad retires. Which I hope isn't too soon, or I'll never keep a job there."

"Keep? Does that mean—"

Fenella's face falls. "My father wants to talk to me about a job," she says in a low voice.

Her words clutch at my heart. "I'm happy for you."

"Are you?"

"Of course I am. If this is what you want."

She looks around as she chews her sandwich with a thoughtful expression on her face. "Why don't you want Wyatt to go to school in Montreal?" she asks instead.

"Who says I don't?" I shoot out.

"I saw your face," she says, very matter-of-factly.

Now it's my turn to look around and decide what to say. I notice a stray cobweb by the window. "It's far."

"Montreal is far from here," Fenella agrees.

"And the world isn't always kind to those who are different." It's the first time I've ever admitted my fear out loud. That Wyatt might face disrespect and prejudice because of his lifestyle. I know he's safe here in Battle Harbour. He's accepted. If he leaves...

"If you mean different like *amazing*, you don't have anything to worry about. Leodie has told me about him, and that kid is impressive. I think he'll be fine wherever he ends up. You shouldn't worry so much."

"Easier said than done," I grumble.

"You're not his father." I look up, but Fenella isn't accusing me. "You're not his father but you've raised him like you were."

"I felt I had to."

"You didn't," she says. "He was your sister's responsibility."

"But she left."

"That's not your fault. It has nothing to do with you. In fact, I think it's best for Wyatt that she did. He might not have turned out as well as he did if he didn't have you and your parents raising him. They clearly did a great job with you."

"I couldn't let them do it alone."

"A lot would have. You gave up your life for him."

"That's what you do for family."

"Not everyone agrees. No one in my family would give up their dream for me."

"That's—"

"Sad? I never really thought of it until I saw your sacrifice. But this isn't a pity party. This is me, in a strange, roundabout way, telling you that Wyatt is very lucky to have you in his life. But you can't keep him here, safe and protected and under your watch. He needs to go and be himself, and you need to be you."

I finish my sandwich, carefully folding up the wax paper. "You're pretty smart for an influencer," I tell her, not knowing how touched I am that she could go right to the heart of things.

I have given up my life to stay here with Wyatt. I gave up my dream of going to the stars. I gave up Mia.

What I take from Fenella is that I don't have to do that again.

A heavy weight lifts off my shoulders.

Fenella

A FTER LUNCH WITH SILAS, I go back to work.

I don't know what it is about him that lets me say whatever I'm thinking. Or feeling. And I never worry about him judging me or thinking less of me.

I can really be myself with him.

I make it to late afternoon, and when I finally lock the door behind me, I can barely walk. Cleaning is hard and my body isn't used to it.

Tomorrow might be rough.

Tonight might be rough, too. When I make it across the square—no longer striding merrily—and up the stairs to Edie's apartment, the rumble in my stomach tells me I need food.

Only there's not a lot of food in the apartment.

I take a handful of crackers and have a quick shower before I head out to the store.

"I'm going for supplies," I tell Ernie. "I'll bring you back something delicious."

It's another first: I've never been grocery shopping in my life.

I've picked up snacks at a Mini-Mart and I'm quite familiar with the various stores where one can purchase alcohol and wine around the world, but I've never pushed a cart around a Food Mart.

I don't even know where to start.

I live at home where there are housekeepers who do this sort of thing—Ada in Los Angeles, Annie in London, and Blossom who makes the best hot bakes in St. Lucia. As far as I know, my mother has never stepped foot in Whole Foods since she married my father.

She had a life before they married, but she never talked about it. Never even alludes to it by mentioning old memories or telling us stories about her younger years. It's like she hatched, perfectly formed, into Adelaide Carrington when she was twenty-four.

She was younger than I am now when she met and married my father. That fun fact always makes me cringe when I think about it, which I do my best not to.

I try not to think about my mother much at all, and the fact that she comes up so often in my internal thoughts really irks me.

I am irked as I push my cart through the aisles of the Food Mart. Because I can hear my mother's slightly patronizing voice in my head, plus I have no idea what food to buy. And I need some sort of food. I can live on take-out for months at a time, but not when there is no Uber Eats in Battle Harbour and only four establishments that let you leave with food.

If I'm going to live on my own, I need to have food in the apartment. If not for me, then at least Ernie the cat.

I stop in the middle of the cookie aisle with a thought: Even if I have food in the apartment, what am I going to do with it?

I can't cook.

My mother never saw fit to ensure I had some of the basic life skills, like boiling water and turning on an oven. In fact, she made it clear to Ada, Annie, and Blossom, that both Ashton and I were never allowed in the kitchen.

I've never understood why, and neither did Blossom, because we had a conversation about it once when she was making me my fresh pineapple juice.

There were always meals available for me at any time of the day, and a pantry full of snacks. There are plenty of snacks in the store, but I can't live on them.

Maybe I can find some ready-made food. I wheel my cart around to the produce section because that seems like a logical place to start.

Jackpot.

I find pizza and chicken tenders and a container of macaroni and cheese that seems a little congealed but looks edible. There are bowls of salads and cups of cut-up fruits and vegetables and I pile it all in my cart.

"Are you having a party and haven't told me?"

I look up with surprise to find Silas beside me with his own cart. Unlike mine, his is full of reusable mesh bags holding brightly coloured fruits and vegetables—not the pre-cut kind—and a sheaf of green leaves that I suspect is kale.

And then I stop investigating his cart and look at Silas. "Hi."

"Fancy meeting you here," he says with a chuckle. "This might be the last place I'd expect to see you."

Silas Bell has a very pleasing mouth. Lips that are not too full, not too thin, but are just right, much like Goldilock's porridge. Wide, but not too big. Teeth that might have benefitted from an extra few trips to the orthodontist and a pack of Crest Whitening Strips but seem perfect to me.

There is nothing about Silas that I don't like, and I usually find something that I don't like.

This scares me almost out of the store.

"I thought the last place would be cleaning a bathroom," I say instead of making a run for it.

Even after a shower, I can't get the smell of the cleaning products off my hands. I added extra moisturizer as well. "I ate all of Edie's crackers and need to find food," I tell him. "Is this what happens in small towns? You bump into people at the grocery store? Because I've never found a friend at Whole Foods."

Silas narrows his eyes. "And how often do you go to Whole Foods?"

"Not very often," I admit. "But look at me. I'm shopping."

He glances down at my selection. "For yourself or the entire town? Because you're not going to be able to eat all that yourself before it goes bad."

I never thought of that. Food only lasts so long. I can always stop here before every meal but that seems like it would be a pain.

"I never like coming here when I'm hungry because I end up buying too much, or stuff that's bad for me," he says.

I wonder what Silas would consider bad for him.

"It's not that I'm hungry—well, I guess I am—but I don't know what to get. What are you buying?"

He gestures to the cart. "I'm making kale and bean soup."

"Sounds good." I'm not sure about the soup, but who knows? Ada has made stranger things.

"Do you know how to cook, Fenella?" Silas asks. He looks like he already knows the answer.

"Not really, no."

He reaches in to take the tenders out of my cart. "They're not good after tomorrow, so I wouldn't eat them. Want me to make you dinner? Teach you a few things along the way?"

He says this without an ounce of patronizing or like he's criticizing.

"Are you serious?"

"About the best before date? Look." He hands me the package.

"No, about teaching me to cook."

"Depends on what you want to cook. I'm okay, but I'm no Michelin-starred chef."

"You know about Michelin stars?"

Silas grins, the relaxed one he uses when he likes someone. A warmth starts in my stomach at the thought of being one of those people. "I watch The Bear."

Because of that warmth, my smile isn't as easy but it gets there, and it's real. "It's a good show. He's really sweet."

If I wasn't watching him I wouldn't have noticed the flash of resignation across his face. "You know Jeremy Allen White, don't you?"

"I've met him a few times," I admit, feeling funny about the confession. My life is all about who you know, but here? Not so much.

"Is there anyone you don't know?"

I glance around. "I don't know the owner of this store, or I would tell him he's got expired food here."

Silas laughs and wheels his cart around. "Let's find you some real food."

SILAS

"WHAT'S YOUR FAVOURITE FOOD?" I ask as we push our carts around the produce area.

"Ravioli with ricotta and lemon and truffles," Fenella says without a moment's hesitation.

Uh-huh. She even says ricotta like a person who's been to Italy more than a few times. "Sounds great. But I think that's a little out of my wheelhouse. I was thinking more like spaghetti and meat sauce."

"Meat sauce?"

"We can call it Bolognese if you like."

"You really want to cook me dinner? You already fed me lunch."

"Would you have eaten if I hadn't?"

"Probably not," she admits.

I had plans for dinner. I was looking forward to cooking and relaxing in front of the television with Wyatt but now, things have shifted and I have offered to cook for Fenella. There will be no relaxing.

But there will be Fenella.

I don't really understand myself. All I know is that there is a rope attached to me and it's pulling me toward Fenella, whether I want it to or not.

"Well, then," I say. "But Wyatt has to come over as well. It's my night with him." I shouldn't want a teenage chaperone, but having Wyatt there might stop me from obsessing over what it would be like to kiss Fenella. And going around and around—Should I kiss her? Should I not?

"And you were going to make him kale soup?" Fenella seems horrified and thankfully unaware of where my thoughts are. "He's sixteen—that's harsh."

"He'll eat anything."

"I won't. But dinner sounds wonderful." And she smiles at me, like the first time I saw her—only better. Because I know her smiles now, and I want them all.

I know I'm making a mistake, but I can't help myself. I keep thinking that if I don't kiss her, it'll all be fine.

I'm not sure about that now.

She stops her cart and fishes her phone out of the huge bag that takes up most of the top of the cart. "What's Wyatt's number? I'm going to invite him over while you grab what we need for Bolognese."

"Sounds good."

"Don't forget the garlic bread," she calls after me.

I know then that having my nephew as a chaperone isn't going to do anything about how I feel about Fenella.

I may have just given her the chisel to begin cracking open my heart.

Whatever I thought Fenella knew about cleaning, I quickly find out that she knows even less about cooking.

But she's eager to learn. Almost excited about it, asking questions about spices and sauce and even the difference between lean and extra-lean ground beef.

I help her select enough food for a few days and load everything in her car for the drive to the apartment.

I park at my place and grab Wyatt, walking across the square to help Fenella finish bringing her groceries up the stairs.

"You're directly across the square from me," I tell her on the last load. I point to the window where I can just make out the green front of Coffee for the Sole in the dim light.

"I know. Don't you be using that telescope to spy on me." Fenella shakes her finger at me with a mischievous grin.

There's another new one.

I hijack the kitchen, instructing Wyatt to finish his homework at the table, Ernie the cat perched on the chair beside him. Then I settle Fenella at the counter with a cutting board, an onion, and a very sharp knife.

"I don't know about this," she says, eyeing the blade. "You brought your own utensils which tells me two things: you know what you're doing, and that knife is probably very sharp."

"Are you afraid to show me your knife skills?" I ask.

"No, I wouldn't be if I had any skills with a knife other than—" She does the Psycho gesture and a *reet reet* sound effect.

"So you think you could stab someone but not cut up an onion?"

"I never said I couldn't, only implied that I don't know how."

"And that's what I'm here for."

I give her detailed instructions on how to cut up an onion, a carrot, and a red pepper. Then I show her how to brown ground beef before we put everything in a big pot, adding a can of tomatoes, garlic and a healthy shake of oregano.

It's fun.

"Leodie said you're having a party." Wyatt watches Fenella as I put a pot of water on to boil, rather than focus on finishing his homework. I can't blame him—I gave her butter and garlic to spread on a baguette, and she seems to be making a concerted effort to cover every last crumb of bread.

"I am. And you're not invited because you're sixteen, and also because I have plans for you," Fenella tells him, not looking up from her garlic-bread duty.

"Plans?" There's no mistaking the excitement in his tone.

"I am in need of some muscle. Would I be able to borrow you and a few of your friends to help me unload some furniture on Wednesday after school? If you don't have practice or a club or a date. I'll pay you," she adds.

"You don't have to pay me. And sure—I don't have anything on Wednesday."

"Great. And of course I'll pay you. Also, I may be in need of servers for the party. It's on Sunday night—you interested?"

Wyatt drops his pencil and the cat pounces. "I can go to the party?" he breathes. "I'm going to a Fenella Carrington party? Oh, my god!" His voice rises with each word until he's shouting. "Yes!"

"You can't touch any of the alcohol, or we'll be shut down before we open," she warns. "And you have to wear all black—shirt and pants. And don't eat all the appetizers."

"Oh my god." My nephew, usually so laid back and *laissez-faire,* is practically vibrating with excitement. "Thank you, Fenella." He pushes away from the table and rushes her with the grace of a linebacker and throws his arms around her.

"You're welcome." She laughs and hugs him back. "You're doing me a favour, you know."

"This is going to be incredible."

"I hope so."

Wyatt seems to have attached himself to her, but just as I'm about to tell him to release, I see the look on Fenella's face.

She looks so happy being hugged by Wyatt. At how excited he is.

We're in Edie's kitchen making dinner. The two of us are making a meal like we do this all the time. It's cozy, it's comfortable.

It's like we're a couple.

And that's when I know Fenella Carrington has crawled into my heart, regardless if I think it's a good idea or not.

Fenella

SILAS MAKES GOOD SPAGHETTI.

He said we made it together, but he did most of it. I burnt the edges of the garlic bread because I was going over the invites to my party with Wyatt.

He's a cool kid.

Silas is...

I'm not exactly sure. He was one thing, but then things shifted—like the tectonic plates shifting in an earthquake—and now he's something else. He was my friend, and then that shifted. I don't even know when it happened.

All I know is that, for the next few days, I spend a lot of time with him.

And I like it that way.

He still hasn't kissed me though, and I'm not sure I should take the plunge myself. Something is holding me back.

The thought of me leaving soon holds me back.

Silas schedules me for the afternoon in the coffee shop, which means I have the mornings to work on party things.

Monday, I go in first thing to finish all the cleaning. Then I work for a few hours in the coffee shop, closing with Silas. After, I meet Sophie Laz next door and the two of us put on the first coat of paint.

Sophie's an artist, so I was right in that means she knows colours and how to paint.

It's a good skill—painting—and like Silas with the cooking, Sophie is serious as she teaches me how to tape doors and light switches. But I know my life. I'll never paint anything again.

My first thought was to paint it all pink—pink walls, ceiling, even the drinks would be pink—and then I had another idea.

I asked Sophie if she could paint it like a night sky.

I don't tell Silas this. I let him help with the first coat of paint, but Sophie has Tuesday off work, and we do the ombre technique to make the walls go from a dark blue-purple to a pale pink on the floor.

Sophie does it. I paint the ceiling purple.

Once that is finished, I don't let Silas inside again. But I have dinner with him that night, and I think not knowing what's going on is slowly driving him crazy.

We go back to the lighthouse to look at the stars.

On Wednesday, Wyatt and three of his friends helped me unload the delivery of the bartop along with the chairs and two fainting couches.

Thanks to Amazon delivering to Laandia, my collection of glassware comes on the same day. On Thursday, Coy Schmidt helps me assemble the bar—or does it for me. The top is a piece of glossy laminate laid across a wall of frosted glass with pink lights behind it to make it glow.

I make plans to borrow Tyler, from The King's Hat, to act as bartender, and thanks to Sophie and Laura Schmidt, the chef at the fish and chips place agrees to work for me for the night, making an easy selection of appetizers.

Langdon is a nephew of Laura's, and while I promised not to poach anyone, I have a feeling he'll make the move over to Hela's, if I can pull this off to make it a more permanent place.

I decided to call it Hela's. She may be the goddess of death, but she's also a badass, with ties to Odin—the original Viking one—and seems to fit in the theme of Battle Harbour.

I keep track of what Coral and Rupe and Milo are doing through social media, but now I scroll through the feeds without the FOMO that plagued me for the first few days.

And some days, I even get to the afternoon without peeking at Insta.

I've never been so exhausted—or so happy.

Planning a party is something I do in theory—I figure out what I want and then tell the right people, who make it happen. Never my mother, or at least not since I was ten and Ashton and I had a joint Cars birthday party and I had a meltdown when we started opening presents and everyone brought Ashton something Cars related but not me.

After that, I would decide what theme I wanted for my birthday party—I never had a joint one with Ashton again until our twenty-first—and I would tell one of my parents' assistants and they would make it happen.

They were good parties; my father liked things perfect, which is why he married my mother, who does appear perfect on the outside. The assistants and the housekeepers organized and planned, setting up and taking down, and even buying me the mountain of gifts that came from being another year older.

But I never did any of the work on these parties until now.

And there is a lot of work to be done.

Once Sophie and I finish painting, I focus on the creaking floorboards by the window and the toilet that keeps running in the men's washroom. I fix the floorboards by laying a parquet square over top to use as a dance floor. Silas got it for me, and it's the perfect size.

Of course, he had it delivered to the door and I wouldn't let him come in because I want the décor to be a surprise for him.

As for the toilet, I jiggled the handle until I broke the chain clean off. The husband of the baker moonlights as a plumber, and I got him to fix it for me.

I've gotten to know quite a few of the storekeepers around the square. I like to think of them as my people.

My father has people to plan his parties and put things in motion, and now so do I.

I think I'm going to be able to pull this off. In fact, I know I am.

There's a funny feeling when I turn off the light before I go home.

It's pride.

SILAS

I KEEP AWAY FROM Fenella when she's not working for me for my own safety/sanity. And because she told me to.

In her words, Fenella said, "I don't want you to see it until it's all ready."

It's three days before her party, and I have no idea what the first floor looks like. Nor am I going to tonight, because it's the annual pumpkin carving evening at The King's Hat.

Prince Kalle and Edie have been hosting this for years: any of the storekeepers in Battle Harbour are welcome to come to Kalle's pub a few days before Halloween and carve one of the pumpkins that Edie's father donates. And then everyone puts their jack-o'-lantern in front of their door to make the downtown more festive.

Fenella is closing with me today. "What needs to be done tonight?" I ask as she wipes the counter.

For an indulged billionaire influencer, or whatever she's called, Fenella has turned into a pretty good employee. Sure, there are times she's on her phone and a customer is standing patiently waiting for her, but she's polite and cheerful and always ready to laugh at herself if she doesn't know something.

The customers have fallen in love with her as quickly as she gains followers.

It's hard to believe she hasn't even been here for two weeks.

Twelve days, and another four to go. And after that...

"I don't have anything to do," Fenella says happily. "I'm buying the alcohol tomorrow, and my lights should be in tomorrow as well. Lots to do tomorrow night, but tonight is wide open."

"Do you want to carve a pumpkin with me?"

"Well, that's definitely a first," she teases.

It's so *easy* with Fenella. We're comfortable, like an old shirt that's been worn and worn until it's almost worn through. But that doesn't mean there isn't a spark.

Or, I think there is. I still haven't convinced myself that kissing Fenella would be a good idea.

I know it would be—parts of my body tell me that. But the rest of me is worried that kissing her would lead to other things, and then with her leaving in days—

I don't like thinking about it. So I don't.

I invite her to carve pumpkins instead.

"Edie's father brings in a truckload of pumpkins from his fields. Did you know he used to be the groundskeeper of the castle?"

"Edie is the daughter of a groundskeeper, and she's eventually going to be the queen of Laandia?" Fenella's arched eyebrows almost disappear into her hair. "That wouldn't happen in most royal families."

"Laandia's royal family isn't like most royal families," I point out.

"I was with you on the dance floor when the king and Duncan did duelling guitars, so I'll have to agree with you. Tell me more about why you're carving pumpkins."

"We get pumpkins, and a group of us get together and carve them, and set them out in front of the stores to decorate for Halloween. Kids around don't go trick or treating from house to house, they come into town and go to the stores, and then there's a party in the square for the older kids."

"That sounds fun."

"It is. It's one of my favourite holidays."

"Halloween always gets mixed in with my birthday, so I never really think of it as a holiday," she muses.

"Feel like going with me tonight?"

Instead of answering, Fenella steps forward to wrap her arms around my waist. She's hugged me several times, and each time, thanks to her footwear, she's a different height. Today she wears flats, so I'm able to rest my chin on the top of her head.

"I want to do as much with you as I can," she says into my chest. "While I still have time."

I tighten my arms around her and hold on for as long as I can.

Fenella

THE LIGHTS ARE ON at The King's Hat.

I've never been inside Kalle's pub when there wasn't a crowd around the bar and the pool table wasn't filled with fishermen talking trash about their catches, storms, and whose boats are the biggest.

The pool table is full, but with pumpkins. A piece of plywood covers the green felt, and at least a dozen pumpkins sit on top.

Sheets of plastic cover most of the surfaces.

"No beer until the knives are away," Edie calls over the din of people greeting each other.

Silas leads me to one of the few booths and I slide in across from him. A pumpkin sits before me, smooth and round and unyielding. Silas sets a knife and a spoon—*a spoon*—before me.

He brought me here because he thinks I fit in with Battle Harbour. The group of twentysomethings who work for a living. Socialize together.

His friends.

Silas brought me into a group of his friends, and I am not going to give him any reason to think that I don't fit in.

I pick up the knife and eying the pumpkin, I stab it.

"What are you doing?"

"Making an eye."

"You have to clean it out first." He looks at me quizzically. "You know that, right?"

"Sure." What exactly am I supposed to clean?

"Fenella." Silas drops his voice. "Have you never carved a pumpkin before?"

My shoulders slump. Why am I bothering pretending that I belong here with these people who know how to attack a defenceless vegetable—or is it a fruit—with a knife sharp enough to draw blood? "Of course not," I say glumly. "We had people for that. Every year, Ashton and I would get a birthday party and there would be tons of jack-o'-lanterns and I have no idea how they came to be, or who even carved or cleaned or whatever it is that I'm supposed to do."

Silas pulls his orange globe closer. "You have to get the insides out before you can create your masterpiece." He takes his knife and carves a circle around what's left of the stem.

"Once it's open, you pull out the guts." He sticks in his hand and pulls out a clump of glistening orange tendrils dotted with seeds. "You can use the spoon for that, but it's better to get your hand in there."

I copy what he did. Maybe my opening is a little bigger than Silas's but it doesn't look too bad. But when I plunge my hand inside— "It's cold," I cry with delight. "And kind of gross." I pull out my hand. "Ew."

"Save the seeds," Silas suggests. "You can roast them."

"Why?"

"They taste good."

"I've had pumpkin seeds in salads, but these look different."

"The pepitas are inside but it's better to roast them like that with a salt. They're good for you. Maybe not the salt."

"You should sell them," I say without thinking. "Roast a bunch and put them in little baggies with a ribbon and sell them at the coffee shop. A pre-Halloween snack."

Silas looks at me strangely. "That's a really good idea."

"I'm full of them."

"Fenella!"

I look up to see Sophie Laz with a pumpkin and knife in hand. "I didn't expect to see you. I thought you'd be doing party stuff." She looks genuinely happy to see me and slides into the booth beside me.

"I've done everything I can do tonight," I tell her. "Silas thought I needed a lesson in pumpkin carving."

He pokes the stab wound on the pumpkin. "Do you blame me?"

"How's the guest list coming?" Sophie asks as she attacks her fruit with a skill that suggests numerous pumpkins have been carved.

"It's over fifty now. I had to cap it at sixty-five, but I'm sure not all of those will come."

"You invited sixty-five people to your party?" Silas sounds choked.

"That's the A list. I could have two hundred and fifty if we had the space."

"The A list," he mutters.

Sophie's eyes widen. "Are a lot of your friends coming? Is your brother?"

"The Brats are, and Ashton. A couple of girls I know from modelling, but I tried to keep to those who won't post every detail all over TikTok."

I had talked to Gunnar about this before he left for his trip. The king had graciously banned all international press from Laandia during my visit, but as helpful as that was to keeping the Fenella fans and haters away, there were still influencers and regular folks who used their phones to get the word out.

Between the two of us, we came up with a list of those who didn't rely on followers or likes to have a good time. I've kept a low profile for the last two weeks, and no one is more surprised than me that it feels amazing not having the world know my every move.

My closest friends will be here, but most of the guest list is made up of those from Laandia.

But I'm not telling Silas that.

I chat with Sophie as I take my time with the pumpkin, freeing all the seeds from the strings before I attack the outside with the knife. My face is basic triangles and a huge mouth that should have had teeth, but like I told Silas, I don't have knife skills.

"What do you think? I turn my pumpkin to face Silas. "My first time."

"I bet you don't say that too often," he says, turning it this way and that. "You seem to have done everything."

"It's surprising how many firsts I've had since I've been here," I admit.

He glances at me with a half-smile. "And has that been good for you?"

Good for me? Since when does anyone ask if something is good for me? I nod. "I think so."

"This looks great." He spins it around to face me.

"It looks like a face, doesn't it?" The eyes are different sizes and the mouth ended up more of a hole, but at least it will show lots of light.

I like it. It's my first jack-o'-lantern.

"It does."

SILAS

FENELLA CARVES TWO PUMPKINS, and the second is much better than the first.

It's always a fun evening, more so this year because I get to watch Fenella try something new.

That was the plan. I'm not trying to change her, only show her what else is available in the world that doesn't come with a price tag only a few can pay.

"That was fun," Fenella says as we wave goodbye to Edie and Kalle. "Thank you for bringing me."

"I have fun with you."

Fenella tucks her arm in mine. "I know."

I like her confidence. And I like when she laughs at herself, and when she admits she doesn't know something.

I just like her.

We leave out the front door and it's an easy walk home for Fenella—straight down the alley. But I don't make the turn. Instead, I linger by the door because I'm not ready for the night to be over. "Are you...?" I stammer. "I thought... Do you want to walk down to the pier with me?"

She tightens her grip. "Are there stars at the pier?"

"There might be a few."

"Then I'm in. I never could have imagined that looking at stars would be something I enjoyed," she admits as I steer us away from The King's Hat.

"It's not that exciting a hobby," I concede.

"It's not that... okay, maybe it is a bit," she says with a laugh. "But I don't do a lot that involves being outside when it's dark in places where I can see the stars. And I don't do a lot that involves me being still."

"I've noticed that about you. You like to keep busy."

"I thought the first few days here would kill me," she confesses with a laugh. "It's so quiet and—"

"Boring?" I offer.

"No." She gives a quick shake of her head. "I thought so at first, but not now. Now, it's... comfortable. I like being here."

"But..."

"There was no but."

"But you're still going home." I shouldn't be frustrated at the thought. I should be grateful for the time she's been here and that I've gotten to know her.

A nice guy would feel that way.

But how is a nice guy—or any guy—supposed to spend time with Fenella without falling for her? Without hoping for more.

"That's where my life is," Fenella says softly.

"And you're happy with your life?"

She doesn't answer. There is a long pause, and I wait for her response until I finally realize it's not coming. I can only assume that she's so happy with her life and her friends and the new job that her father will give her, and I can't compete with any of it.

How could I think I could compete with anything?

"Show me the stars?" she asks.

I can do that.

It's a short walk to the pier. Some of the fishing boats are in for the evening, but some are out for days or weeks at a time. Waves lap at the hulls, rocking them like a baby swing and lick at the wooden pier jutting out to the sea. The air smells like salt and fish and... pumpkin.

I smell like pumpkin. So does Fenella.

I slow my steps to make the trip out to the end of the pier last longer. The air is colder this close to the water and the odd wave sends a splash of water across the boards, but stars are best seen as far from the light as possible.

"Tell me about your friends," I invite. Knowing how important they are to Fenella, how influential they must be in her life makes me a little nervous about meeting them.

More information on them might help, or it might lead to an anxiety spiral about how I'll never be good enough to be a part of her life.

It really could go either way.

"Have you heard of them?" she counters. Her arm is still in mine, and she brushes against me like she's hunting for warmth.

She wore her toque tonight and a new, warmer coat she bought with Edie. The pink pom-pom bounces against my shoulder when she gets too close.

I don't mind. I don't think Fenella could ever be too close.

"I know there's a group and you seem to move as a pack." Like hyenas, I ponder, but don't share that opinion with Fenella. I don't know her friends—I only see what they put out for the world to see in their posts and ads.

"They... understand," she says slowly. Warily. "What it's like."

"Being you?"

I hear her exhale, almost like she was waiting for me to say something else. Something negative, or judgmental. "Kind of. I sound horrible when I say this, but being me hasn't always been easy."

I put my hand over hers. She might have brought a hat but neither of us remembered gloves, and her fingers are cold under mine. "You got exiled from your home because the world is obsessed with your life. I can't imagine that being easy at all."

"Yes." Fenella's sigh is one of relief and sounds like air escaping from a tire. "You get it."

"Not really, but I can try to understand."

"Most people don't try. They just write me off for having the most perfect of lives. Listen to me." She shakes her head.

"I hate complaining about it, but if I do, my friends would understand. Coral especially—her parents own this winery and half of Napa Valley. She had to fight to work there too. No one else works; Lavinia and Milo are models, and that's where I met them."

"That's considered a job," I point out.

"Lavinia's father is an earl and has some relation to the royal family and Milo's family owns half of England. It's not exactly a job when you don't have to do it."

"Is working for me not a job?"

She looks up with a smile. "Working for you is fun. And I needed something to do or I would have been climbing the castle walls."

"Well, I'm glad you convinced me to hire you," I tell her.

"I don't think I have to work very hard to convince you," she says, dropping her gaze, only to look up through her web of eyelashes.

"Maybe not." I feel like I'm being hypnotized. Caught up in a spell where there are only the two of us here. Entranced by Fenella and her—

There are so many things that fascinate me about Fenella, but it's the entire package that has me caught up in this moment—the dichotomy of what I know about her and what the world assumes.

The mask she wears and what she's really like.

Fenella laughs softly, then gasps. "Falling star!" A flash of light curves down the sky.

"Meteor, maybe. It's hard to tell without a closer look."

"Let's call it a falling star so I can make a wish."

I don't tell her wishes are usually made while the star is still in the sky. If Fenella wants to make a wish, who am I to argue?

"What's your wish?" On the end of the pier, I turn to face her, my arm sliding around her waist almost of its own accord.

"I'm not supposed to tell you." Her gaze slips to my mouth.

"Am I allowed to guess?"

"You can try."

This is the moment. This is the very moment that I've been running from since I met Fenella and now, instead of running, I'm leaning in.

I lean down and brush her lips with mine, so gently it's barely a touch.

"That's kind of what I wished for," Fenella whispers, her mouth inches from mine.

"Only kind of?" Without waiting for a response, I put my hand on her neck, stroking my thumb over her strong jaw. I focus on her lips for a moment, so glossy and pink, and then I kiss her.

I kiss Fenella Carrington.

And she kisses me back.

Her lips part under mine, and a noise, soft and sweet, escapes. Her arms wind around my shoulders and she clutches at my jacket. I cup the back of her head and lean into the kiss—into her.

There's no running.

I was so stupid to think I could run away from this.

Fenella

S ILAS IS KISSING ME.

I want to add *finally*, but with a kiss like that, I shouldn't add anything but a fireworks emoji, along with a flame and maybe my head exploding.

And many, many hearts.

He's kissing me on the pier after the star fell from the sky—or maybe it was a meteor. I really don't care, only that it led to this moment. the moment I've been thinking about for a week now.

Silas. Kissing. Me.

I could have done it days ago. I wanted to. I was ready to. But it had to be him to make the first move.

And it was. And, oh my god, the man can kiss.

At first, it was gentle, almost tentative, with lips as soft as they look. And then, after what might have been a practice lap, he really makes his move. Instead of asking, he demands, and then he takes.

I'm along for the ride because I do my share of taking as well.

We stay on the pier until my fingers are numb with cold, so Silas takes my hand in his to warm it as he walks me home.

The lights of The King's Hat have dimmed when we walk by and when I look in, I see Kalle and Edie by the pool table.

Dancing.

The two of them in a bubble of happiness and love, ignoring the rest of the world.

That's what it felt like when Silas kissed me.

I've kissed my fair share of men. The movie star when I was nineteen, embarking on a whirlwind trip around the world with him, only to discover his interest in me was only to further his career. The athletes, the musicians, the Bitcoin golden boy.

The prince of Laandia.

What I felt for Gunnar was most like what I'm feeling for Silas and I have to wonder if there's something in the water of Laandia.

He walks me through the alley to the door of the apartment, the only part of staying at Edie's that I don't like. But with Silas holding my hand, I want to dance through it, hopscotching over the cardboard boxes and bits of paper the wind has thrown around.

"I had fun tonight," I tell him as we pause before the door. "Thanks for taking me."

"I'm always happy to give you another first," he says, holding my gaze in his green eyes. His cheeks are pink from the chill and his lips—

His lips look a little swollen, thanks to me.

And there's a bit of a burn on my cheeks from his beard.

"I really enjoyed that last first one." And I take his coat and pull him closer, standing on my tiptoes to press my lips against his again. "The one that started like this."

He wraps his arms around me, holding me upright when my knees threaten to buckle.

Silas makes my knees weak.

He gives me butterflies.

My pulse is racing, my heart is thumping. Silas gives me all those things that kisses are supposed to do, and he does them all at once.

He makes me smile.

He sees me smile, and it makes him happy.

I'm so happy kissing him.

We stand there for long minutes, wrapped up in each other, until I can't feel my toes. And then it takes us another ten minutes to say goodnight.

"Don't forget to look for your pumpkins tomorrow," Silas says, backing away from me. "They'll be out in front of the stores in the morning."

"I'll go on a scavenger hunt to find them," I promise. "On my way to work."

"Tomorrow."

Tomorrow is the last shift I have scheduled, but I don't want to bring that up now. I don't want to break this bubble. "Tomorrow," I repeat.

I keep my eyes on Silas as he walks away, and only when he's out of sight, do I head up the stairs to where Ernie the cat is waiting for me.

Once I peel my coat off, I pick up the cat and hug him, because I have to do something.

I text a picture of my pumpkins to the group.

> Me: I lost a nail in my attempts

> Coral: Carving pumpkins? What did they do to you?

What did they do to me? This place—this small town with the decent men who make me happy.

I've kissed royalty. Billionaires, millionaires, and rock stars. I've kissed men who appear on the cover of Men's Health and People's Magazine and have more Instagram followers than even I do.

I've never kissed the boy next door, and I think that's what Silas is. I've never kissed a man who is so devoted to his family that he would let his heart get broken rather than deserting them.

I've never helped repair a broken heart.

I've kissed some men, and it's gone nowhere. I've kissed others, and they asked me to marry them.

I feel quite confident with my kissing skills.

But it's different with Silas.

Butterflies. Fireworks.

Shooting stars.

I text my brother.

> Me: What if I stayed?

> Ashton: Why would you want to?

> Me: It's nice here. Peaceful. Calm.

> Ashton: You are not calm. Who is he?

> Me: There's no one. It's a sweet place.

> Ashton: You are not sweet. Or calm. You are tough. Vivacious, vibrant

> Me: Are you running through the V words in your thesaurus?

> Ashton: I'm trying to be nice here.

> Me: And it never happens so I really don't know how to respond.

I don't tell anyone Silas kissed me. I hug it to myself like I hugged him and spend the rest of the night trying to come up with a plan.

SILAS

I DIDN'T SLEEP WELL last night. Or the night before, and definitely not the night before that because the memory of kissing Fenella kept me awake. If I went to sleep, I might think it had been a dream.

Only it wasn't.

Last night, it was the heaviness of dread that kept me tossing and turning.

Gunnar and Stella had returned home yesterday with a plane full of people and swept them up to the castle. Fenella had worked until noon and then disappeared to greet them.

I told her she didn't need to take her shift, but she wanted to. I'm not sure if, like me, she's counting down the hours until she leaves.

She didn't work today; yesterday was her last shift and the knowledge hangs heavy in my chest.

I haven't been looking forward to her party because once it's over, she'll be gone.

Fenella led her pack into Coffee for the Sole about an hour ago. They were like a gust of very expensive air blowing through. Every one of them was beautiful, but Fenella glowed the brightest of all.

"Hi." She had smiled at me, and the walls regrowing around my heart had cracked a bit. "Everyone? This is Silas, my—"

"Boss?" I suggested.

She shook her head, eyes shining like purple crystals. "My friend. My very good friend."

"Who you happen to like kissing." I'm not sure who said it, but Fenella laughed as I flushed red. Apparently, they are a very close group who share personal details.

"You're not supposed to know that, Milo," Fenella chided, but didn't seem too upset. "Silas, this is Rupert, Coral, Lavinia, and the loudmouth is Milo. That's Mase, his wife Fiona, Tad and Demi. And this—" She drew a handsome man forward who shares her features. "This is my brother Ashton."

He extended his hand and I could feel the scrutiny. "Good to meet you," Ashton said. It's easy to see they are siblings, but while Ashton is model attractive, he lacks the spark Fenella has.

Or maybe it's the purple eyes. Ashton's are a dark blue.

I said hello, answered a few questions about Battle Harbour, and took their orders. Leodie made most of their orders and I tried to give them for free, but Gunnar insisted on paying.

Stella gave me a sympathetic smile as they filed out to head next door.

The music starts at four o'clock. The thump of the bass, the laughter of Fenella and her friends getting next door ready for the party tonight has me gritting my teeth.

For once, I close Coffee for the Sole early. I had thought Fenella might need help but when I texted her to see if she needed anything, she told me everything was great and she'd see me at eight.

The many exclamation points she uses leave me with a bad taste in my mouth.

It's not like Fenella is ignoring me, or even avoiding me. She's texted me constantly since the night of the pumpkin carving when I kissed her.

She kissed me.

We kissed.

I'm not opposed to others knowing about it, but I know I'm going to look like an idiot if she leaves without saying anything.

I don't even know when she's leaving. Her meeting with her father is Tuesday so she should fly home Monday with the rest of them.

Her friends, who are currently spending time with her, while I stand next door, filled with self-doubt and unease and everything else that is going to make it hard to walk into her party.

We kissed, and I want more.

But I don't think I'm going to get it. I should have known.

"Silas?" I turn, suspecting it's not the first time Leodie has called to me. She and Jem are waiting by the door. "You okay?"

"Yeah."

"Dude, what are you wearing tonight?" Jem asks nervously.

I glance down at my flannel shirt and jeans. "Dunno."

"Not that, I hope?" Leodie rolls her eyes. "It's a big night for our little town. You have to look your best."

I have no idea what my best is, but even if I did, I know it wouldn't compare to what Fenella's friends will be wearing.

I lock the door behind Leodie and Jem and head into the back to check through the resumes on file to see if there's someone I can contact for an interview.

I got Fenella a present—an annotated book on the night sky and a small telescope that looks like an old-fashioned spyglass.

I ordered it the night after I showed her Neptune.

The floor of my apartment vibrates from the music downstairs as I shower and trim my beard, make myself something to eat, and then find something suitable to wear.

It's harder than I expected, and I change three times. The ironic part of it is that I'm trying to impress Fenella but if I called her, she would be able to tell me exactly what I should wear.

I finally decide on black pants that may not be the latest style, but they look okay, and a black button-up shirt that Edie gave me a few years ago for a gift exchange and that I've never worn. It has silver threads woven in.

It takes me two shots of whiskey to get me moving.

I've never been nervous in social settings, but my feet feel like they're stuck in mud, unable to move down the stairs. I hate feeling like this—like I'll be walking straight into the worst that can happen and I won't be able to stop it.

I wanted to be there right at eight, but it's not until a quarter after that I head down the stairs to enter through the kitchen.

The place is packed already with bodies dancing to loud music. I catch sight of Wyatt as he winds his way through the crowd with an empty tray. "Hey," he shouts over the music. "What do you think?"

I don't know what to think.

I expected a crowd, not Mrs. Geordie, Nancy Tanker and Laura Schmidt in the middle of the dance floor with Milo and Duncan Laz, shaking it with everything they've got. Or Coy Schmidt leaning against the bar having a serious heart-to-heart with Ashton Carrington. Or Prince Kalle and Mase Stirling chatting in the corner with Wyatt's coach—I recognized the billionaire baseball player when he came in earlier—while Edie and Mase's wife fangirl over what Lavinia is wearing.

Which isn't much—a dress that is more like a roll of bandages wrapped around her body in Big Bird yellow, with shoes to match.

There are so many I recognize from town, people that I had no idea Fenella knew.

I hover by the kitchen door and take it all in. Sophie catches my eye and hurries over as fast as she can wearing four-inch heels and a tight black dress, her reddish-brown hair pulled up into a messy bun and with more makeup than I've ever seen her wear.

"Silas," she cries, a pink cocktail in her hand. "What do you think?"

"You look amazing," I manage.

"No, your club." She laughs. "But thanks."

It was supposed to be pink. I expected pink, pink everything, and while the furniture and most of the drinks are of a pink hue, the walls are... not.

"She wanted to surprise you," Sophie says, leaning in so I can hear her. "She was so excited about the idea."

The ceiling is dark blue, almost indigo, and the colour works its way down the walls fading into a lighter blue, violet, lavender, and pink a few feet from the floor.

It's the night sky, soon after sunset, just like the sky by the lighthouse. The ceiling and top of the walls are full of stars—silver pinpricks and sparkly shapes dangling on wires.

"Do you like it?"

So engrossed in the sight of the place, I don't even see Fenella come up to me. But once I see her, I don't know how I could have missed her.

She's wearing silver, a strapless matte tube of fabric that starts at her chest and hits mid-thigh. It's not tight but manages to accentuate every curve on her body.

My mouth dries up at the sight of her.

"It's…" I pull my gaze from her and slowly turn in a circle. "What happened to pink?"

"I wanted this. For you."

"It's supposed to be for your birthday."

"This is how I wanted it to look. It's like a gift for you." Her eyes shine as brightly as the amethysts in her ears and around her neck.

I've never seen anyone look so beautiful.

"Thank you," Fenella says.

Apparently, I said that out loud.

"It's the sky you showed me." She points to a spot on the ceiling across the room. "That's Neptune."

That's Neptune.

I can only stare at her, and she laughs with delight. Someone calls to her and she waves them away, her gaze fixed on mine. "Do you like it?" she demands.

Instead of answering, I reach out for that slim, silver waist and crush her and the dress against me. And then I kiss her.

In front of all her friends and the whole town, and knowing tomorrow is going to hurt more than I think I can bear, I kiss Fenella Carrington in the middle of her birthday party.

Fenella

I DID NOT EXPECT that reaction from Silas.

I'd hoped for it, but I didn't expect it and now I'm kissing him back even as my smile widens across my face.

Silas shifts, his lips pausing in their assault against mine.

A nice assault.

"Stop smiling," he growls. *Growls*. I never knew he could make that noise, and the sound thrills my insides.

"I can't help it." I bury my face against his neck and hug him tightly. "I'm so happy you like it."

"I'm so happy I let myself like you," Silas says into my hair.

I pull back and look at him. At his warm green eyes—they look more hot and a bit hungry rather than warm right now—and the softness of his beard. I touch his cheek. "You trimmed."

"I had to look my best for you."

"I don't need your best," I tell him. "I only need—"

You, but I don't say it.

"I like you more than I should," Silas says.

"Me too," I admit.

I realize we're blocking the kitchen when Wyatt tries to slide by, and I take Silas by the forearms and move him behind the bar. Tyler nods at him but leaves us alone.

"I like you, too." I say it out loud, for anyone to hear. "Maybe even—"

More? It's definitely more than like, but I hadn't wanted to admit it because it happened so fast, and when things happen fast for me, they tend not to work out.

But it feels right with Silas, like he is the puzzle piece I was missing.

And with that kiss, it clicks into place.

"I'm falling in love with you," Silas says loudly, loud enough for Tyler to glance over his shoulder at us, and for Rupert standing at the bar with Mabel Crow, to widen his eyes at me.

He gives me a thumbs-up.

"I wanted to say it first," I tell him, my smile creasing my face in a way that will make my cheeks ache, but I don't care. Silas *loves* me and I love him— "I'm falling in love with you, too. Just wanted to get that out there."

I'm smiling and ecstatic, happiness bubbling out of every pore, and Silas—

Silas looks like I kicked his puppy. Not a good look when the man you love just expressed his love for you.

"That doesn't make you happy?" I demand. "It makes me very happy, and it's my birthday, so you need to be happy too."

"Your birthday." Silas blinks. "Happy birthday, Fenella. You look incredible." He leans down and brushes my forehead with his lips.

"Nu-ugh." I shake my head at him, the ends of my hair flying in a curve. "I want a kiss like before."

"You're going home." His sadness is palpable.

"Yes."

His shoulders slump. "You're leaving."

"I didn't say that."

Silas's brow furrows, and I can't help but smile because confused Silas is quite adorable. "I don't want you to go."

"I know. We'll talk about it later." I take his hand. "If you're not going to kiss me, then dance with me. Let's have fun. Please, Silas?"

He shakes his head. "I can't say no to you."

"I know. You need to remember that."

My twenty-seventh birthday party is one to remember.

My closest friends are here, and my brother, and new friends I've made. I invited everyone I have ever interacted with from Battle Harbour, and almost every one of them came, most of them bringing friends, so the sixty-five guests are more like eighty, and we have to prop open the front door, letting in the cool air and allowing people to spill out onto the street.

This acts as an invitation to others walking by, as well as those who live on this street or close enough to hear the music, and so even more people stop by.

I do my best to talk to everyone there. I dance with Silas but eventually lose him in the crowd, only to find him deep in discussion with King Magnus and Kalle, with Spencer hovering.

I do shots with Coral and Sophie and leave them to have a giggling conversation about my brother.

I hug Coy Schmidt when he leaves with Laura, avoid a hug from Jonathan McKibbon, and take a selfie with Nancy Tanker.

We run out of food by eleven o'clock, and Tyler pours the last of the vodka just after midnight.

"So we're going to have to work on having more of an inventory and crowd control," I say to Silas. It's after one, and the majority of the crowd has dispersed, mostly after they realized we were out of alcohol.

"We?" The music has slowed from the frantic dance beats and I sway in the middle of the floor with Silas.

"We. Your club, my club, the bar that we should open. You have to admit, after this, Hela's is exactly what Battle Harbour needs."

"Hela's? The goddess of death?"

"Maybe she just had a bad day. It happens, you know."

Silas smiles, but it quickly fades. "I agree that *Hela's*—we'll work on the name—would be a good idea; but Fenella, you have to know that if I open something, I'd want you to run it."

"I know. We'll talk about it later."

"When later?"

"Tuesday."

SILAS

NOT LONG AFTER THAT conversation, Fenella, with Gunnar's help, closes the place up. I stay to help clean up as much as I can, hoping I can have some time with Fenella when the others leave.

But she leaves with her friends, taking the bottle of peach schnapps that Tyler missed, and climbing into one of the SUVs to take them back to the castle.

She kisses me good night, tells me again that she'll see me on Tuesday, and gives me a big smile as they drive away.

The next day, I find out she's gone.

Fenella

I CAN'T BRING MYSELF to say goodbye to Silas.

I don't even tell him I'm leaving.

After the party, I go back to the castle.

The next morning, Gunnar arranges for cars to the airport and for flights to get everyone where they need to go. He flies a group back to New York and then continues to Costa Rica, with a few stops on the way.

Ashton, Milo, and I take a flight to St. Johns, and then onto London so I can talk to my father.

My brother takes the seat beside me in first class. He falls asleep instantly and I stare at the screen where some movie is playing, trying to decide if this is really what I want.

I keep thinking of Silas and the expression on his face when he finds out I'm gone.

Ashton wakes up as we begin to circle Heathrow. "Hey," he mumbles.

"Wakey, wakey, Sleeping Beauty."

"Yeah." He yawns and I hand him my bottle of water to help with his morning breath. Afternoon breath. I'm not even sure what time it is in London. "That was a cool party last night."

"Why don't you ever want to have a party?"

"Why bother, when I can let you do all the work—" He yawns again and gives his head a shake. "I need some of that coffee your boyfriend makes."

"Silas isn't my boyfriend."

"Sure looked like it last night."

"I don't know what he is."

Ashton glances sideways at me. We've always been close, despite our different lifestyles. It's always been him and me together on one side, and our parents and Evan on the other. "But you want him to be something."

I don't say anything.

Ashton shrugs. "He's a better dude than Tiger, that's for sure. What about that Sophie girl?"

"What about her?" I ask suspiciously. Other than a brief fling with Coral, Ashton has never been interested in one of my friends. And it is interest in his voice that I hear—just like he knows there's more I'm not telling him about Silas.

I'm not sure how I feel about this.

"What's her story?"

"You'll have to figure that out by yourself," I tell him curtly. "I'm not about to play matchmaker."

"Yeah, you're not very good at it."

"I am so."

We don't say much else until the plane lands. "You going straight to see Dad?" Ashton asks.

I nod, already trying to pull up the Fenella I need to be to deal with our father. That Fenella seems very far away from the Fenella I've been for the past two weeks.

The Fenella I've become. In only two weeks, too. Battle Harbour has been good for me, in my opinion.

Let's see if my father agrees.

SILAS

I GET A TEXT from Fenella late Monday afternoon, the first I've heard from her since Sunday night.

Sunday night when I told her I was falling in love with her. But even more amazing, Fenella told me she felt the same way.

It doesn't seem real, because if it was true, why would she leave without saying goodbye?

> Fenella: I couldn't say goodbye to you. I'm sorry. But I'll see you Tuesday night.

She ends it with a heart emoji, which is something but she doesn't say where she'll see me, or how. Fenella just pulled off the party of the decade in Battle Harbour, and that's including a royal wedding. I wouldn't put it past her to be able to send a hologram of herself to me tomorrow.

Monday morning was slow but picks up to a packed house in the afternoon as all the sleepy and hungover townsfolk file in for some much-needed caffeine.

It's good to keep busy, but bad because all anyone wants to talk about is Fenella.

I let Leodie man the cash register while I keep the pumpkin spice lattes coming.

It hurts that she didn't say goodbye. It hurts just as much as I thought it would. But I manage to keep a little flicker of hope alive.

I'm falling in love with you, too. Just wanted to get it out there.

Tuesday is Halloween, and by noon, anyone with young children has given up on a normal workday. The City Council spends the afternoon readying the square for the party that night, and I ready myself to see Fenella.

Only the afternoon turns into the evening; trick-or-treating begins and I start to hand out pumpkin-shaped cookies that my mother spent all week making. Mini Marvel characters, part of the Paw Patrol, princesses and fighter pilots shriek as they run from store to store collecting treats.

Beside Coffee for the Sole, Hela's stays locked and dark.

I last until nine o'clock. By then, the little kids have finished their trick-or-treating and have been bundled off to bed and the teenagers are dancing in the streets. I see Wyatt with his friends, with Brody, and wave as I head to my car.

I drive to the lighthouse, feeling strange that the bright headlights of Fenella's car are not right behind me like last time.

Maybe she's not coming back. Maybe that's how she works—blowing into town like a storm, disrupting lives and hearts, before leaving, like a falling star.

One minute it's there, and gone the next.

I take the path through the woods, noticing one of the solar lights is burnt out, and set up my telescope. But instead of peering through it, I tilt my head and look up.

The sky is a canvas of dark purple, with pinpricks of starlight, much like the ceiling of Fenella's club. The Draconids meteor shower is odd in that it happens earlier in the night, just as darkness falls. Tomorrow will be the optimal night to watch, but there may be some tonight.

The waning moon helps. And there—I hold my breath as a line of brilliance arcs across the sky, leaving a trail of colour to fade into nothing.

I've seen a lot of things in the sky, but this is magical.

I wish I had someone to share it with.

"Silas!"

I freeze at the sound of a far-off call. I must have imagined it because—

No .Leaves crunch as someone hurries along the path. "I don't like this path by myself," she calls.

Another flash, a line of stardust, but I turn as Fenella bursts out of the trees.

"I knew you'd be here," she says.

Even in the dark, she's a beacon of light in her pink puffy coat and toque with the huge pink pom-pom. And she heads straight for me to throw herself into my arms. "I missed you," she breathes into my chest.

"What are you doing here?"

"I told you I'd be back."

"But why did you leave?" I don't have to ask; I know she left to talk to her father about the job with the family company. What I really want to know, is if she got the job, why would she bother coming back?

"My father offered me a job," Fenella tells me matter-of-fact-ly like she didn't spend the last two weeks hiding out in another country for the chance to work for Carrington Toys. "I told him thank you, and I'd be working remotely, from here."

"*What?*"

She cups my cheeks. "Did you really think you could get rid of me that quickly?"

"But you left." My emotions are pinballing, and I don't know what's coming next.Yes, I may have kept a little hope, but I thought I'd lost her. I couldn't see a way for Fenella and me to work when everything she wanted was somewhere else.

"I had to talk to him in person," she explains. "I'm sorry I ran out like that, but if I didn't go then, I wouldn't have gone at all. I hated to leave you, especially after my party, but I had to."

I'm falling in love with you, too.

I keep her words at the forefront of my mind. "What did he say?"

"Look at that!" Fenella gasps, pointing over my shoulder.

I glance back in time to see the fading line. "It'll be better tomorrow."

"But it's good now."

"Fenella." Her eyes widen at the sharpness of my tone. "You told me you loved me, then ran out of town without another word. *Please* tell me what's going on."

There's no remorse in her gaze; rather she looks like she has a secret. One she's quite proud of. "I went to talk to my father about buying your building," she admits with a hint of a smile. "Hela's building, not Coffee for the Sole. And the one beside it."

It takes a moment for me to respond. "Why?"

"I have ideas for Battle Harbour. Plans that will help tourism, help business for everyone. I really want to make Hela's into a club, like I told you, only bigger. That's why I bought the place beside it—Mr. Pollack is ready to retire and maybe the town doesn't need a pawn shop."

"You already bought it?" I demand. It feels like the ground underneath me is unsteady, like I'm getting too close to the edge and sliding down into the unknown.

She nods. "I did the deal with your parents during the flight. I charted a plane so I could get back in time. I asked them to let me tell you. You can stay in your apartment," she adds quickly. "I'm not kicking you out. Only if you want to—you can take over Edie's place if you want. I bought that building, too."

"What are you doing? You can't just buy the whole town?" The thought of it makes me angry, at Fenella's arrogance that this is what Battle Harbour wants. It's a small, quiet town—it doesn't need to be Fenella-ized.

But... I like the idea. I like the idea of her *here*. Being a part of the community.

"I'm not. But it needs more. I spoke to King Magnus and Kalle, and they both want to go ahead with your idea of an observatory. They want to meet with you to make plans."

"*What*?" Every time I think I understand, Fenella veers off and presents me with more.

"There's going to be a place for people to watch this." She spreads her hands wide. "Learn about this. And people are going to come and watch and learn, and the town needs to prepare. Another restaurant. Hela's. Places to stay. I bought that house on Second Street and I'm going to make it into a bed and breakfast. The apartments in Edie's building and over The King's Hat will be Airbnbs. KingMagnus agrees that there should be a motel outside town." She shrugs and when I don't say anything—when I can't say anything—she keeps going. "I made a plan of the town, of what it could be without changing its character, and Magnus loved it. So did my father. He hired me as a consultant, to look for opportunities to move Carrington Toys forward."

"I don't understand." Restaurants and Airbnbs and a motel? An observatory?

"I want to stay," she says simply. "And so, I made it possible. Not just so we can be together, but for me, too. This place is good for me. You're good for me."

She bought the town because she thinks it's good for her. That I'm good for her.

I have to agree with her. Maybe she's not that different when she's away from here, but I do like her when she's here. And I know I'm not the only one. Her plans might not be what I would have come up with, but the outcome will be the same.

Fenella isn't leaving and that means we've got a chance. And I think it's a pretty good one.

I laugh. It's the only thing I can think of doing, other than kissing Fenella.

I do that, too.

Pulling her close, even as the sky lights up above us, I kiss her with everything I've got—every bit of wonder and gratitude and admiration, of all the relief that she's here. Back with me.

I kiss her for a long time, so when we finally part, the sky is dark, with only the stars as company.

"We missed it," Fenella says, snuggling into my neck. She kisses my jaw. "I wanted to see the meteors with you."

"We'll come tomorrow," I promise. "That's the night to see it."

"It's a date." I feel her smile against my skin. "This is what you should have been doing," she says. "Bringing women up here and—no. Scratch that. You should never bring anyone up here but me." She tilts her head back with a grin.

"I'm fine with that." I kiss her softly. "What I want to know is when did you get the ideas for all of this?"

"It's surprising where your mind goes when you're cleaning," she admits. "I might try it again some time."

I laugh, and kiss her again.

One last meteor flashes through the sky. Or it might be a falling star, but I don't bother making a wish.

I've got everything I want right here.

EPILOGUE

SIX MONTHS LATER

T HE GRAND OPENING OF the new and improved, and larger, Hela's isn't for another month, but I do a soft launch and host Edie's bridal shower two days before the royal wedding.

Only women are invited, just like I imagined, and we have an amazing time.

In the months since I moved permanently to Laandia, Battle Harbour hasn't gone through a massive transformation, but the changes have begun.

Waves, a new Maritime steakhouse, will be opening in another few months, and Valhalla, the new bed and breakfast, is already full of guests for the royal wedding.

Laura Schmidt runs it for me.

Along with my new businesses, King Magnus has taken to scheduling monthly meetings with me, to pick my brain about what else Laandia could use. He talks about putting me on the payroll, but I haven't agreed yet.

Apparently, being an influencer has taught me to look outside the box for new opportunities.

Ground will break for the observatory next year, and Silas has been part of all of the planning. He's very happy about it.

He's not very happy when I drop my shoes.

My heels clatter onto the floor, and Ernie the cat ricochets off the couch. "Fenella?" Silas calls sleepily from the bedroom.

"Sorry!" I giggle because having an amazing time with a group of women involves a great many shots and pink cocktails.

I hear his chuckle. "Was it fun?"

"So much fun." Because he's awake, I stop trying to be quiet, and when I enter the bedroom, I flop on the bed beside him. "I missed you, though."

"I doubt that, but thanks." His arms wrap around me and I snuggle in.

Life with Silas hasn't been a great transformation, but it has changed me. I gave up my influencer sponsorships and rarely go on social media now, especially since I hired Wyatt to manage my accounts. He knows my brand as well as I do.

I also give him a ten-thousand-dollar bonus when he serves at Hela's for me, to help pay for his tuition when he goes to school in Montreal. It pays to be a billionaire.

Even though it doesn't pay very well to work at Carrington, my father pays me a consulting fee, and when I brought my latest ideas to him—a line of toy cars marketed toward girls as well as a racing school for women—I also asked for a raise.

I'm headed back to Los Angeles after the wedding.

And this time Silas is coming with me because he decided he can't be without me for the week I'm away.

I hoped that would happen because I didn't want to be without him.

It's a lot of fun being a billionaire these days.

Want more Fenella and Silas? Sign up for my mailing list for a BONUS SCENE, plus you'll get all the news about when my next book is coming out!!

Sign up here!

And then get ready for Babysitting the Grumpy Billionaire!

(Can you guess who's story this is??)

READ THE SERIES!

READ THE REST OF the Cinnamon Rolls and Pumpkin Spice Series!

Each book is a standalone, full-length, closed-door romance that can be read in any order.

Hating the Cinnamon Roll CEO by Camilla Evergreen

Falling for Autumn (Again) by Jen Atkinson

Paris, Pumpkins & Puns by Marion De Ré

Fall With Me by Amanda P Jones

Cinnamon & Spice Conundrum by Leah Busboom

Cinnamon Roll Set Up by Genny Carrick

Coffee Break with the Billionaire by Holly Kerr

The Friendly Fall by Kristine W Joy

THANK YOU!

WHEN I JOINED THE Cinnamon Rolls and Pumpkin Spice group, I had been working on the second book in my Love in Laandia series. I had already decided I wanted a spin-off for Fenella (and possibly her Billionaire Brats friends—stay tuned) so it was a no-brainer that she would be the star of this one. And Silas? If there was a picture of a cinnamon roll hero in the dictionary, it would be Silas Bell.

I'm sure every author thinks that, but I *really* believe it. He's just so *nice* but not in a boring way. At least I hope you find him the same!

Thank you to the authors in the series with me: to Camilla, who came up with the idea and pulled us together, to Marion and Kristine who came up with so many of the marketing ideas, to Genny, who stepped in late, but pulled it off, and to Leah, and Amanda and Jen for their support and encouragement and ideas. This has been a great ride and I'm so glad I was able to take it with you!

Thank you to Regina and Kaitie, all my eagle-eyed ARC readers, and Blu. And thanks to Indie for the cover—love the cover!

Thank you to my children for their support and understanding for a mother who needed to finish four projects this summer in between trying to spend as much time with you as I could, along with cottage visits, baseball games, and getting everyone off to university. I think I've finally recovered.

But most importantly, thank you to my readers,—whether you have just discovered me, or have followed me from a Las Vegas wedding-that-didn't-happen to the country of Laandia. There may be some of you who have been here since my Canadian super spies days, and those who want more sisters in small towns.

Thank you for reading Coffee Break with the Billionaire!

Holly xo

READING LIST

Love in Laandia

Royal Rumble
Royal Retelling
Royal Rising
Royal Reluctance
Royal Rebel

Suitor Science

Hating the Chemistry Teacher
Falling for The Suitor
Fraternizing with the Ex
Marrying the Billionaire Best Friend
Loving the Wrong Guy
Finding the One

Don't

Don't Tell Me You Love Me
Don't Want to Be Friends
Don't Stop Me Now
Don't They Know It's Christmas

Love & Alliteration

Perfectly Played
Beautifully Baked
Pleasantly Popped

Charlotte Dodd

The Secret Life of Charlotte Dodd
The Missing Files of Charlotte Dodd
The Best Worst First Date Ever
The Hidden Past of Pippa McGovern
The Last Stand of Charlotte Dodd

Sisters in a Small Town

Coming Home
Hanging On
Stepping Up

Unexpecting
Unexpectingly Happily Ever After

STANDALONES

Cinnamon Rolls and Pumpkin Spice - Coffee Break with the Billionaire

Oceanic Dreams - I Saw Him Standing There

Absinthe Doesn't Make the Heart Grow Fonder

ABOUT THE AUTHOR

WHEN SHE'S NOT HUDDLED in her writing cave, Holly likes to rewatch Ted Lasso and all the Marvel movies, attack the weeds in her many gardens, and watch her son and daughters play baseball, which has led to a side gig as a softball coach for the last ten years. She prefers beach over mountains, won't touch coffee, and likes her martinis dirty, with extra olives.

If you happen to pass by her house in Toronto during happy hour, she'll invite you onto the porch for a glass of wine and a chat about what's in her Little Library.

Visit her at:
www.hollykerr.ca
Facebook – @hollykerrauthor
Instagram – @hollykerr.author